Caught Up in the Drama

Other titles in the Good Girlz Series

Caught Up in the Drama

ReShonda Tate Billingsley

Gallery Books

New York   London   Toronto   Sydney

Gallery Books
A Division of Simon & Schuster, Inc.
1230 Avenue of the Americas
New York, NY 10020

First Gallery Books trade paperback edition April 2010

GALLERY and colophon are trademarks of Simon & Schuster, Inc.

For information about special discounts for bulk purchases, please contact Simon & Schuster Special Sales at 1-866-506-1949 or business@simonandschuster.com

The Simon & Schuster Speakers Bureau can bring authors to your live event. For more information or to book an event, contact the Simon & Schuster Speakers Bureau at 1-866-248-3049 or visit our website at *www.simonspeakers.com*.

Manufactured in the United States of America

10 9 8 7 6 5 4 3 2 1

Library of Congress Cataloging-in-Publication Data

ISBN 978-1-4391-5686-5
ISBN 978-1-4391-7077-9 (ebook)

To Ms. Lillie Lacy,
My seventh-grade English teacher, who helped me nurture and develop a love of the written word.

Caught Up in the Drama

1

Alexis

I so could not believe my eyes. That was actually my girl, my best friend, up on that stage, and she was on fire! She sounded like Beyoncé, Rihanna and Ciara rolled up into one.

I wasn't the only one who was shocked. I glanced over at my other best friends, Jasmine and Angel. Both of their mouths hung wide open as well.

"Did you know Camille could sing like that?" I whispered. We were at the Search for a Star talent show, and we'd been real nervous ever since Camille had announced she would be singing instead of dancing. That's because we'd had no idea she could sing that great!

Angel shook her head, leaving Jasmine to reply. "I mean,

she's always humming and singing some song, but I had no idea she could blow like that."

Not only were we stunned at how totally fierce Camille sounded but I think we were also a little hurt that she could sing like that and none of us had known it. After all, we'd been best friends since joining the Good Girlz two years ago.

The Good Girlz was a community service group formed by Rachel Jackson Adams, the first lady of Zion Hill Missionary Baptist Church. It was just four of us—me, Jasmine, Angel and Camille. Miss Rachel had started the group as part of a youth outreach program. Even though her daddy was a preacher, Miss Rachel had been buck wild as a teenager, and she'd wanted to do something to help teens who were headed down the wrong path like she'd been.

A lot of people hear Good Girlz and think we're some Dolly Do Right type of girls. Shoot, I wish. Try as we might, trouble just seemed to follow us around. First, Camille had gotten in trouble because she'd hidden her thuggish convict boyfriend at her grandmother's house. She thought he'd been released from jail, but the fool had broken out, and Camille had gotten arrested for "harboring a fugitive." That's why she'd come to the Good Girlz. It had either been that or juvie.

Jasmine had joined because she'd always been fighting. She came from a big family and had grown up that way. She'd been kicked out of so many schools because she used to have a bad attitude. I say used to, because my girl really made progress over the last year. Granted, she would still tell you off in a minute, but she was a whole lot better than she used to be.

As for Angel, she was the quiet and sweet one of the group.

Getting pregnant at fifteen made her grow up pretty fast. Her mom made sure she lived up to her responsibilities, but she was holding her own, especially now that her triflin' baby's daddy had decided to help her take care of their daughter, Angelica.

Everybody liked to tease me as "the rich girl of the group" just because my daddy owned a couple of hotels and we lived in an eight-thousand-square-foot home. They just don't know that I'd trade all the money just for some of my parents' time. They both were so busy, especially my dad. But that's a whole other story.

Not only were we in the Good Girlz together but now we all attended school together at Madison High School. After weeks of begging and pouting, I'd finally gotten my parents to agree to let me finish my senior year at Madison with my friends. I had gone to a private school called St. Pius, and since I'd already received an early acceptance letter to three colleges and finished all of my required coursework a year early, they'd let me transfer so I could graduate with my friends and enroll in extracurricular activities that we didn't have at St. Pius.

That was the best move I could've ever made. Not only was I having so much fun on the drill team with Camille but all four of us were growing tighter. We'd been through a lot together, and we knew each other inside and out.

At least I thought we did.

"Does my boo look good or what?" Xavier's voice snapped me out of my thoughts.

I had been so caught up that I had forgotten about Xavier Gant, Camille's new boyfriend. All four of us had come to watch Camille in the citywide talent show. We knew she could dance. After all, she was the captain of our high school drill team. But when she'd announced yesterday that she was going to sing instead, well, let's just say we'd immediately had visions of those people who suck on *American Idol*. And since we hadn't wanted our girl to be the one they talked about on the radio the next morning, we'd tried to talk her out of singing. But Camille had just grinned slyly and told us to trust her.

I guess when you have a voice like that, you can have all the confidence in the world.

". . . and you're gonna love meeeeee!" Camille finished up her song, bringing the crowd to their feet. I mean, folks were going wild. Camille actually sounded better than Jennifer did in *Dreamgirls*, and I'm not just saying that because she's my best friend.

We snapped out of our trance and started cheering wildly along with everyone else.

"That's my girl!" Jasmine shouted from our third-row seats.

Camille smiled confidently, but she wasn't cocky. She just had a glimmer in her eye that said she knew she had rocked it.

We didn't waste any time. All of us, Xavier included, took off backstage.

"Girl, I cannot believe you!" I squealed. She looked so cute, standing there looking like the actress Kyla Pratt. She had her hair in cute ringlets that hung to her shoulders. Her layered rhinestone tee and cropped jacket blended together perfectly with her skinny jeans.

"Yeah," Jasmine echoed. "How come we didn't know you could sing like that?"

"It's just a little somethin', somethin' I do," she said playfully.

"There wasn't anything *little* about that, babe," Xavier said, leaning in and giving her a big bear hug. "That was off the chain!"

"I'm serious," I said, playfully pushing her shoulder. "What's up with not letting us know you had it goin' on like that? I mean, we've only been your best friends for what, two years?"

Camille shrugged. "Y'all know dancing is my thing. I just never really thought much about singing." She looked lovingly at Xavier. They'd been dating for three months now, and Camille swore he was the one. But then, every boy Camille dated was "the one."

"It was actually Xavier's idea," she continued. "He heard me singing and pushed me to enter the singing part of the competition instead of the dancing."

We all turned to Xavier, who looked even prouder than we did. They looked perfect together. They both were the same smooth chocolate color, with flawless skin and athletic builds. But I didn't know whether to be happy or a little ticked that he knew something about our girl that we didn't. I decided to let it slide.

"Well, you won the show, hands down," Angel said.

"I hope so." Camille crossed her fingers. "Do you know what I would do with a thousand dollars?"

Both Jasmine's and Angel's eyes lit up. Both of them pretty much came from struggling families, so a thousand dollars was a big deal.

"Hey, I think they're about to announce the winners," Jasmine said, pointing at the emcee, Nnete, a local radio personality from 97.9, who was leaning over to get an envelope from the three judges at the table in front.

"You got this," I said, giving Camille a quick hug.

All her confidence was gone now. Camille was literally shaking. Xavier wrapped his arm around her waist as she clutched her hands in front of her mouth, no doubt praying that she'd win.

I held my breath as Nnete called the third-place winner, some strange-looking girl who'd sounded okay singing Jazmine Sullivan's "Bust the Window Out Your Car." When they announced that second place was going to a group that had sung an old Boys II Men song a capella, I relaxed. Because as good as they were, they still didn't have a thing on Camille.

"Before I announce first place," Nnete continued, "I have a very special announcement. You all knew that the winner of tonight's talent show was going to get a thousand dollars." She paused as the crowd cheered. "Well, not only will they get that money, but . . ." She paused again for effect. "Are y'all ready for this?"

"I wish she'd go on already," Jasmine huffed.

"How many of you guys have heard of Sisco?" Nnete asked.

The crowd went wild. That was a dumb question. Everybody in Houston knew who Sisco was. Shoot, everyone in the country knew who he was. He was only the hottest young rapper out there. His first album had won two Grammys. He was popular not only because, at six-feet-two, with a washboard chest, light hazel eyes and wavy hair, he was fine as all get out, but he had also made a name for himself by not being all over the top with his raps and by staying out of trouble. He didn't curse or talk dirty, but he still managed to spit some tight rhymes. He was a proud Houstonian and was always boasting about H-town.

Nnete was just about to say something else when a voice from the other side of the stage said, "Awww, that's all the love y'all got for me?"

Right then, Sisco walked out from the wings. I swear I thought everyone was going to bum-rush the stage, Angel and Jasmine included.

After security pushed everyone back and got the crowd to calm down, Sisco continued. "Dang, y'all, chill." He laughed. "We still gotta announce the winner." He gave the crowd a minute to settle down. "I know some of you are wondering why I'm here," he said when it was quiet enough for him to continue.

"We don't care why you're here, we're just glad you are!" someone screamed.

"I love you, Sisco!" someone else yelled.

"I love you back!" Sisco said. "But I'm here tonight to help announce the winner of tonight's talent show and tell her, or him, that in addition to the money, they are going to get to perform a cameo in my video that we're shooting in two weeks right here in H-town."

Once again the crowd broke out in a frenzy, and Angel, Jasmine and I were screaming right along with them. Camille stood there frozen, too stunned to speak. She loved Sisco, knew every song he'd ever written, so I could only imagine what must've been going through her head.

"I know you guys are tired of waiting, so let's get to it." He took the envelope from Nnete. "The winner of tonight's talent show, and the person who will be appearing with yo' boy in my next video, is"—he read the paper—"Camille Harris!"

We jumped up and down, screaming and hugging each

other. I had to quickly catch myself when I noticed Sisco looking around like he was searching for Camille. "Girl, go," I said, pushing her toward the stage.

Camille didn't need much prompting. She ran onto the stage and dang near jumped into Sisco's arms. If I hadn't been so happy, I probably would've been embarrassed that my girl was acting a fool like that. But under the circumstances, I was going to give her a pass on that one.

As Camille posed for photos with Sisco and the other winners, we couldn't contain our excitement. I don't know how long we'd been going crazy, but I finally looked over at Xavier, who was standing off to the side of the stage by himself. He was the only person not smiling. As he carefully watched Sisco's every move, I could tell that he wasn't too happy about Camille's win.

2

Camille

$\mathcal{I}$ could not believe my boo was standing here acting all stank. It was his idea that I enter this contest. Now he had his lip stuck out like he was mad.

"Xavier, what is the problem?" I asked. "You act like you're upset about me winning." Dang, he was killing my joy. My girls were excitedly waiting in the car for me. We were going over to my house to talk to my mom. I knew I needed to at least try to see what put Xavier in such a foul mood. Right about now, though, I wanted nothing more than to throw him the peace sign and jet over to my friends.

"Camille, I don't have a problem with you winning. I have a problem with that fool grinning all up in your face. Every picture he took, he had his arm around you."

I took a deep breath. I had been so excited about the chance to work with Sisco that I hadn't even thought about Xavier. "But you like Sisco. He's one of your favorite rappers."

Xavier ran his hand over his closely cropped fade. "I know. I mean, shoot . . ." He frowned. "Why you gotta be all up in his video?"

That had to be the dumbest thing I'd ever heard Xavier say. Who wouldn't want to be in Sisco's video? This was the chance of a lifetime, and I wasn't about to spoil it because my boyfriend was all insecure. I looked over at Jasmine, Alexis and Angel laughing about something as the music thumped in Alexis's BMW. That's where I needed to be—celebrating my win with my girls, not over here trying to pacify Xavier.

"Look, babe, it's no big deal," I said, standing on my tiptoes to kiss him on the cheek. "I'll call you later, okay? Jasmine has to be home by eleven and we still have to go by my house."

"But . . ."

I didn't give him time to respond as I waved 'bye and bounced toward the car.

He stood there looking pitiful, but I would have to deal with him later. Right now it was time to celebrate.

"Dang, I must really be hot stuff. Y'all left the front seat for me," I said after sliding into the passenger seat.

Jasmine reached up from the back and playfully pushed my head. "Don't get beside yourself, though."

I giggled as I leaned back against the headrest. It had been a long night, but I wouldn't change one thing.

"So, what was Xavier trippin' about?" Alexis asked as she carefully pulled out into traffic.

"Yeah," Jasmine said, leaning forward. "At first he seemed happy about you winning, but when Sisco came onstage, his whole attitude changed."

I rolled my eyes. I had been so caught up in the excitement of meeting Sisco that I hadn't even thought about Xavier trippin'—it had caught me totally by surprise.

"Yeah, he doesn't like the idea of me doing the video with Sisco," I moaned. "But whatever. I'll deal with him later. For now, I've got to get my mom to sign this."

I held up the permission slip Sisco's producer had given me. Because I was underage—only seventeen—Sisco's record label said I had to get my parents' permission. They didn't want any problems. My dad died when I was fourteen, so it was just me and my mom. Although we'd gotten a lot closer over the last year or so, I didn't know how she'd feel about me being in a video, even if Sisco was the hottest rapper in the country. But if she wouldn't agree to it, I would just have to convince her. No way could I pass up an opportunity like this.

I said a little prayer all the way home.

When Alexis pulled up into the driveway of my small brick house, everyone turned to me.

When I didn't move, Alexis asked, "What are you waiting for?"

"I'm not ready for this," I replied.

"Girl, please. Your mom is cool." Alexis started climbing out of the car. "Besides, even if she wanted to go off, she's not going to do it with us here."

"Yeah," Jasmine echoed as she climbed out of the back-seat, "unlike my mom, who would just cuss all us out."

Thinking of Jasmine's mom brought a small smile to my face. "Okay, let's go."

I led the way to my front door. After letting myself in, I found my mom sitting in the living room in her favorite spot—her old rocking chair. Her Bible was spread out on her lap. I smiled as I noticed her sleeping soundly. She must've really been tired if she didn't wake up when the door opened. I swear, sometimes I felt my mom had supersonic hearing.

"Hey, Ma," I said, gently shaking her shoulder.

I had played down the talent show because I hadn't wanted my mom fawning all over me and embarrassing me. Besides, I'd known she'd have had to take off from work, something we couldn't afford for her to do.

"Hey, baby," my mom said as her eyes fluttered open. "Hey, girls," she added when she saw everyone else standing behind me.

"Hi, Mrs. Harris," they all said in unison.

"How did the talent show go?" she asked, closing her Bible.

"I won, Mama."

"That's wonderful," she replied as she stood up and hugged me.

"Yeah, Ma, can you believe it?"

"Of course I can," she said lovingly.

"Camille was so off the chain," Alexis chimed in.

"For sheezy," my mother joked.

I groaned in horror, the smile leaving my face. "Mother, please. Don't ever, ever say that again."

My mom laughed. "I heard someone say that when I was flipping through the channels earlier. I thought that was the hip stuff all you teens like. Anyway, are you guys hungry?"

"No, Mom. Can you sit back down?" I said as I glanced nervously at my girls. They gave me supportive looks, so I continued before I lost my nerve. "Okay, so you know I get the thousand dollars for winning, right?" I said when she didn't bother to sit back down.

"Yes, and we're putting that up for college. You can take a hundred and buy you something, and we have to put some in church, but the rest is going for college." She put her hands on her hips like she was readying for an argument.

"Yeah, yeah. That's cool," I quickly replied.

My mom's left eyebrow immediately went up. "Okay, what's going on? Because there is no way that you agreed so easily to only get a hundred dollars. What do you want?" My mom knew me so well.

I flashed a bright smile. "Okay, well, there was a surprise guest at the talent show, and he announced that not only was the winner gonna get the money but they would get the chance to appear in his video."

"What kind of video?" my mom said, instantly apprehensive. "And who was this surprise guest?"

"Sisco. And it's his new rap video. He's shooting it in two weeks."

My mother cocked her head and gave me a look. "I'm sorry. I thought you just said you want to be in a rap video."

"She did," Angel piped in.

I looked at Angel to tell her to shut up. I just needed them here for moral support and so my mom would maintain her cool in front of company. I didn't need them adding to the conversation.

"And this Sisco fella," she asked slowly, "is he one of them gangsta rappers?"

"No!" I exclaimed. "He raps and sings. Kinda like Nas."

"Like I know who that is. Well, the bottom line is, I'm sure you told them you wouldn't be able to do that. Because there's no way my daughter is going to be in some gangsta rap video, where they're bragging about shooting police, forty-inch rims and calling women derogatory names."

Jasmine giggled at my mom's reference to forty-inch rims, but I wasn't in a laughing mood. "Mama, it's not like that. There is some clean rap out there, and Sisco is one of those clean rappers." That was true for the most part. With the exception of a song called "The Freaks Are Out," Sisco stayed pretty clean.

My mom wasn't convinced. "Doesn't he have a tattoo?"

I rolled my eyes in frustration. "That doesn't mean anything," I whined. "He's the biggest rapper in the country, and I have a chance to be in his video with him."

"That would've been nice . . . if you were someone else's child." My mom waved me off as if to say the discussion was over. "But congratulations on winning." She patted my cheek as she headed into the kitchen.

Alexis shot me a look and whispered, "Go after her."

I motioned for them to follow me. "Mom, listen," I said as we all followed her into the kitchen. "Seriously, Sisco doesn't curse in his raps. That's why he's so popular."

My mom turned toward me and wagged her finger. "If you think that I'm goin' to be okay with my only child being a video vixen, you got another think coming."

My mom really needed to turn off the TV. How did she know about video vixens? "I would be singing, not just some dancer," I protested.

She stopped for a moment, like she was thinking. "You'd be singing?"

"That's what I'm trying to tell you. I would be singing a duet with Sisco." I stepped closer. With the best puppy dog look I could muster, I continued, "Mama, this is a once-in-a-lifetime chance."

"Mrs. Harris," Jasmine said, stepping up next to me, "Camille can blow. For real. I mean, she shocked all of us."

"And I have all of Sisco's songs on my iPod," Alexis said. "I could let you hear them so you could see that Sisco really is one of the good guys."

"And I'm sure they're not going to have her in any skimpy clothes or anything," Angel said.

My mother sighed like she knew she was going to have to at least hear me out. "Well, exactly what would you be singing?"

"One of his songs," I said, guessing, because what else would I be singing? "Please, please, please, Mom. Say yes. Because I'm under eighteen, they won't let me do it without your permission."

My mother looked like she was thinking about it. Finally, she said, "Now, how am I supposed to look Reverend Williams in the face with him knowing my daughter is in a rap video?"

That was an easy question. "He'll be proud that I'm not out in the streets robbing and killing people," I said with a wide grin.

"You wouldn't be doing that regardless of whether you were in a video or not." I stuck out my lip in a playful pout, but she scoffed. "That's not working. Do I have to give you an answer tonight?"

"I told the producer I would call her tonight and tell her." I'd met with Sisco's manager for a few minutes after the show, along with two of his producers. They'd all seemed nice, although one of them, a young woman named Taraji, had seemed irritated the whole time.

"Well, can't that producer wait until tomorrow?" my mom asked. "It's already late."

"I can't wait!" I cried. "I'm gonna go crazy if I have to wonder all night long whether all my dreams are going to go up in smoke." Okay, so I was being a little dramatic, but whatever worked, worked.

My mother, who knew me all too well, smiled slyly. "Okay, Miss Drama Queen." She blew a defeated breath. "Fine, you can do it, but only after I hear some of the songs he sings on Alexis's me-Pod."

I groaned at my mother's corny attempt at humor.

"I'll bring it by in the morning on the way to school," Alexis quickly interjected.

"Okay. I can't stand the idea of listening to that rap crap, but I just want to make sure he's not one of those gangsta rappers."

"He's not," Angel said again.

"We'll see."

"Yes!" I squealed, jumping up and hugging her. "Thank you so much, Mom!" Jasmine, Angel and Alexis jumped up and down with me.

"But there will be no rump shaking in this video," my mother warned.

"I don't even know what a rump is," I replied playfully.

"Okay, play dumb if you want to," she said, "but if this

isn't tastefully done, it won't be done at all, understand?" She gave me the look to let me know she meant business.

"Yes, Mother. Yes, yes, yes, I understand!" I kissed her again. "I'm going to walk my girls out."

"'Bye, Mrs. Harris," my friends sang as they followed me out. They were all just as happy as I was.

My mother just didn't know. She'd made my day. No, let me correct that—she'd made my life!

3

Alexis

I was so anxious to get home. Sonja was our longtime maid, and today was her last day. My dad had promised to come home from work early so we could have a nice farewell dinner as a family. Getting my dad to leave work for anything almost took an act of God. That man was a workaholic, with a capital W. But I guess you didn't own a hotel, a bunch of real estate and keep us living in this seven-bedroom house by not working hard.

Still, I would give it all up just to have some of my father's time.

"Hey, Sonja," I said as I walked into the kitchen. Sonja was actually more than a maid. She was like part of our family, since she'd been with us since I was two years old. Unfortunately, today was her last day because she was moving back to Guatemala to take care of her sick mother. So dinner was to say good-bye to Sonja and let her know how much we'd miss her. I'd bought her a nice sterling silver charm bracelet and written a long letter, which I planned on giving her before she left.

"Hello, Alexis. How was school today?" she asked, immediately bringing me an ice-cold glass of lemonade.

I set my backpack in the kitchen chair and took the glass. "It was good," I said. "My friend that won the talent show—"

"Camille?" she asked.

I smiled. Sonja knew what was going on with my friends better than my own parents did. "Yeah, Camille," I nodded, taking a sip of my drink. "I just hope she doesn't get bigheaded."

Sonja looked confused. "I don't understand," she said. "Bigheaded? Her head is growing?"

I laughed. "It's just a saying. Her head isn't growing, like literally. I just don't want her to let the fame go to her head."

Sonja nodded, although I could tell she still didn't understand what I was saying. I decided to change the subject. "Where's Mom?"

"Upstairs, resting." She leaned over to me, smiled and whispered, "She's worn out. Your mother doesn't do well in the kitchen."

I groaned. "So she really tried to cook the dinner all by herself?"

"Not only did she try," Sonja said as she pointed at the ceramic dishes on the counter, "she succeeded. Shrimp Alfredo, black walnut salad, asparagus and . . ." Sonja paused and looked around the room. "You ready for this? Chocolate cream pie!"

I gasped. "No way!"

Sonja nodded. "Yes, way." I knew she was impressed. I think this might have been my mom's second time cooking a meal the entire time Sonja had been with us.

Sonja's eyes watered up. "I am just so touched. That your mother would do something that she hates so much, for me."

I gently touched her hand. "She wanted this night to be special for you."

"I know, but it's her special day, too. Her birthday. Still, she wouldn't even let me help. She wouldn't let me do any-thing all day." Sonja held out her hands. "Do you know she had someone come to the house today and give me a mani-cure, a pedicure and a massage!"

I loved seeing Sonja so happy. "That's because she wanted you to know how special you are to all of us."

"I'm going to miss you all so!"

"Not as much as we're going to miss you," I said. And I meant that. I was just about to ask her what time my dad was going to be home when she let out a loud sob. "I'm so sad!" she said before racing from the room.

I couldn't help but smile, because I was sure that was the first of many tears tonight; she was going to like my gift, but she was going to flip when she saw what my parents were giv-ing her—a check for ten thousand dollars.

I knew she was going to try to return it, but Sonja was worth every penny. Not only had she cared for me and my sister, Sharon, who was autistic and now lived in a special home, but she was also the glue that held my family together. I was no fool. It was obvious that my parents hadn't been happy for a while, but things had gotten really bad the past couple of months. My dad was working late almost every day, and when he was at home he and my mom were at each other's throats. I tried to stay out of their way as much as I could. If it hadn't been for Sonja, I probably would've lost my mind.

I made my way up the winding staircase and peeked into my mother's suite. As Sonja said, she was resting peacefully, a black satin mask covering her eyes. I eased the door closed and went on down the hall to my bedroom.

I told myself I was just lying down for a few minutes, but I awoke to the sounds of screaming coming from my parents' bedroom.

I sat up in my bed and rubbed my eyes. I was shocked to see that it was dark outside. I glanced over at the clock on my nightstand and freaked when I saw it was almost nine o'clock. "Our dinner!" I exclaimed, jumping up. I couldn't believe no one had come and woken me up.

I stopped just outside my parents' room. I was about to knock when my mother's voice let me know why no one had bothered to wake me up.

"Just one time! Can you just put your family first one time!" my mom was screaming. "We sat and waited for you, and I don't even know why we bothered!"

"Calm down, Veronique! You said yourself that Alexis was asleep. And Sonja said she understood."

"Sonja always says she understands, and she doesn't. I don't understand. Your daughter doesn't understand. We don't understand how you can't seem to find any time for anything but your stupid job!"

"This stupid job is why you are able to live in an eight-thousand-square-foot house! This stupid job keeps you in those designer clothes and rolling around in luxury vehicles." His voice dropped as he went on. "You know what, I'm exhausted.

I'm sorry Mr. Carter decided at the ninth hour that he wanted to finish this deal tonight. I'm sorry you slaved in the kitchen—for once."

"You're sorry, all right!" my mother yelled.

By this point I'd had enough. It's like no matter how hard we tried, we couldn't do anything together anymore.

I didn't even realize I was crying until I felt the tears wetting my cheeks. I headed back to my room but stopped just outside the door. I turned and headed back downstairs and didn't stop until I was in my usual place of comfort—snuggled up next to Sonja in her bed.

4

Camille

As captain of the drill team at Madison, I was already pretty popular, but winning the talent show took that to a whole different level.

Everyone was standing around in the courtyard when my mom dropped me off for school. I had barely gotten out of the car before people started racing over to me.

"Are you really going to be in a video with Sisco?" this girl from the drill team asked me.

"Oh, my God, I saw you at the talent show. "You were off the hook," another girl said.

I smiled, replied graciously and tried my best to act like the attention was no big deal.

"Miss Harris, I'm very proud of you." That came from

our mean assistant principal, Mr. Hudson. "You make Madison look good." He had a pleasant expression on his face, which was definitely a change from the scowl he wore the rest of the time.

I thanked him and made my way to my locker. I was tripping off all the people that were smiling and coming up to me. Even the haters were giving me my props. I had to fight back my smile when I saw Dee, this snobby girl I couldn't stand, hanging nearby with her snob squad, as I called them. I knew Dee was hating all of the attention I was getting. That's not to mention her itch for Xavier, my boyfriend.

"Take a picture, it lasts longer," Jasmine said to Dee. She huffed, rolled her eyes and stormed off, her girls in tow.

With Alexis and Angel, Jasmine approached me at my locker.

"What's up, superstar?" Alexis said, giving me a playful bump.

"Girl, trippin' off all the love," I said, pulling my advanced literature book out of my locker.

"I know, right?" Alexis said, delighted at my success.

"You deserve it, Camille. You were so good," Angel added.

"Thanks, guys." I shut my locker. "Honestly, I surprised myself. I mean, as much as I love dancing, I always felt like I could sing, but being up on that stage, it's like someone else took over my body."

"Yeah, Jennifer Hudson took over, that's who." Angel laughed.

We chatted some more before the bell rang for first period. I had been hoping to catch up with Xavier, because he hadn't answered my phone calls last night. I knew that meant he was still mad. We had second period together, so it looked like I would have to wait until then before I could talk to him.

I made it through first period, even though my mind was somewhere else. By the time second period rolled around, I couldn't wait to see Xavier. I wanted to throw my arms around his neck when I saw him walk into the classroom. He looked so cute in his Madison basketball letterman jacket and some baggy Sean John jeans. But of course, I couldn't be seen jocking any guy, even if that guy was my boyfriend. So I had to play it cool and wait until he took his seat.

"Hey," I said as he slid in the desk in front of me.

"What's up?" he replied without looking my way.

"Are you still mad at me?"

"I ain't mad," he replied coldly.

"Then why do you have a funky attitude?"

"I don't have an attitude," he said with plenty of attitude.

"Come on, Xavier. I don't want to argue with you," I whispered.

He reached down and pulled out his history book. "Camille, I'm not . . . oh shoot!" he exclaimed.

"What?" I asked.

"I forgot to do this homework," he said frantically, pulling out his worksheet. "Dr. Reed is going to kill me."

"It's not that serious."

"Yes, it is." He groaned. "She has to fill out my progress report for Coach today. If I don't have this, she's gonna give me an F, and Coach isn't going to let me play in Saturday's game." He looked like he was racking his brain trying to figure out what to do. "Maybe if I sneak out before class starts, I can come back after class and turn it in," he said, almost to himself.

I checked through the window out into the hallway, where Dr. Reed was standing talking to another teacher.

"Or maybe you can just copy my answers," I said, holding out my homework toward him.

He hesitated like he didn't really want my help.

"Boy, would you take the paper? You don't have time to be all prideful."

He sighed and took my paper. He quickly started copying the answers. I was pretty good about my schoolwork, and I could count on one hand the number of times I had cheated in high school, but this was a special exception.

"Done," I whispered just as the bell rang. Dr. Reed walked into the room and announced that everyone should pass their homework to the front of the room. I had made two of his answers different from mine so it wouldn't look like we'd cheated. All innocent, I put our papers on top of each other and passed them up to Xavier.

"Thanks," he said, taking the papers and turning around in his seat. "I owe you."

"I know how you can make it up to me," I whispered behind his ear. "Stop being mad at me."

I knew he wasn't trying, but a small smile crossed his face. "Deal."

I giggled and ran my hand over the back of his smooth fade.

"Miss Harris, can you save the flirting until after my class?" Dr. Reed chastised.

I rolled my eyes and leaned back into my chair.

"And do you need to take that eye-rolling to the principal's office?" she asked.

"Dr. Reed," said this pimply-faced girl named Donya,

sitting in the front row, "don't you know Camille is a big star now? She's gonna be in a video with Sisco."

"I don't care if she's starring with Madonna, Prince and Barack Obama. She will have some respect in my classroom." Dr. Reed stood at the front, her arms folded across her chest, the look on her face telling me she meant business.

"Sorry," I muttered, looking down at my book.

I don't know how I made it through the class, but I had never been more happy to hear a bell ring. I gathered up my things and beelined toward the door. I didn't even wait for Xavier. I would just wait outside in the hallway. I had just reached the door when I heard Dr. Reed say, "Miss Harris, can you hang back a minute? I need to talk to you."

I groaned as several of my classmates flashed "better you than me" looks as they headed out the door.

"Yes, ma'am?" I said, approaching the front of her desk.

"One minute."

She waited until the last student had left the room before turning her attention back to me. "Miss Harris, do you want to tell me what's going on? That eye-rolling? That's not like you at all."

"I wasn't rolling my eyes," I protested.

"Oh, so I guess I'm just crazy, huh?"

I wanted to tell her yeah, but I wasn't crazy either, so I remained silent.

"Camille, you are one of my best students," she continued. "I would be remiss if I didn't warn you not to let fame go to your head."

"Huh?" I said. "I just won the talent show yesterday."

"I know that. I'm not saying that you have let anything go

to your head yet. But you are too bright, too sweet and too levelheaded to get beside yourself, and I just wanted to give you a warning from the very beginning."

I gave her a reassuring, yet fake, smile. "Thank you, Dr. Reed. But seriously, me letting this video go to my head? I don't think so."

"I hope so, Camille."

"I know so, Dr. Reed."

She nodded like she knew better. "Okay, go on to your next class."

She didn't have to tell me twice. I hurried out the door. Me, getting beside myself? I was as grounded as they came. That was the last thing anybody had to worry about.

5

Alexis

I could not believe my eyes. Camille was blinging from head to toe. She had on a cropped House of Deréon jacket, with some matching jeans. Crystals ran all up and down one leg and across the back of the jacket. She had on a tight baby doll tee with the word "Diva" spelled out in crystals across the front. She'd waltzed into the Good Girlz meeting late, with some gigantic Super Fly glasses on. But the thing that had our mouths open was the wild chestnut-colored weave hanging down her back. It had only been three days since she'd won the talent show, and she was already getting the big head. I glanced over at Jasmine and could tell she was about two seconds from telling Camille about herself.

"Hey, you guys," Camille sang as she slid into the chair behind me. Miss Rachel, who had been at the front of the room talking about today's lesson, shot her a disapproving look.

Not bothering to hide her frown, Jasmine surveyed Camille's appearance. "Your mama called."

"What?" Camille asked, looking confused.

Jasmine pointed to her head. "Your mama called. She said to tell you make sure you bring her mop home after the meeting."

"Oh, you got jokes," Camille laughed. "You can't tell me I don't look fly." She fluffed her weave.

"Really, I can," Jasmine said, turning back around in her seat. "As if the outfit isn't bad enough, how many horses had to die for you to get that hair?"

Camille patted her hair again. "Number one, it's one hundred percent human, and number two, I'm trying a new look," she said. "I sewed it in myself."

"I would hope you didn't pay anyone for that," Jasmine said. "If you did, let me know who they are so I can make sure I never go to them."

Camille was starting to get a little testy. "It's not like you go to the beauty shop anyway. All that pretty hair and you keep it up in a ponytail," she muttered. "But maybe if you save up all year, you can get a weave like this."

No, she didn't go there. Camille knew Jasmine was sensitive about being poor. I needed to stop her before she said something that really set Jasmine off. Luckily, I didn't have to, because Miss Rachel stepped in.

"That's enough, girls," Miss Rachel said. "We only have an hour, and we are not going to spend it bickering."

We'd been in the middle of our weekly Good Girlz lesson when Camille had come strolling in. The meeting had started twenty minutes ago.

"Nice of you to join us, Camille," Rachel added.

"No problem."

Rachel paused, then motioned toward Camille's glasses.

"Oh," Camille replied, "you like?" She fingered the glasses. "My future is so bright I gotta wear shades." She laughed.

"You are soooo corny," Jasmine huffed as me and Angel giggled.

Miss Rachel sighed heavily. "Girl, take those glasses off. It's bad enough that you come up in here late, then you want to act like you're some kind of diva."

"Miss Rachel, haven't you heard?" Angel chimed in. "She's about to be a superstar."

"About to be ain't the same as is," Miss Rachel snapped as she walked over and removed Camille's glasses herself. "And even if you are a superstar, show some respect for the House of the Lord."

We all giggled as Miss Rachel got on Camille. She needed it. She'd been trippin' at school for the last two days. I knew she was loving all the attention she was getting, but I hoped this was just a phase she was going through.

"Anyway, where were we?" Miss Rachel asked, returning to the front of the room.

Angel raised her hand. "We were talking about how you shouldn't judge a book by its cover."

We'd actually been having a good discussion before Camille had sauntered in.

"That's right," Miss Rachel said. "And Camille is a prime example of that. If you didn't know her but just looked at her outer appearance, what would you think?"

We all turned to Camille.

"Why you gotta use me as an example?" she whined.

"I would think she's a prima donna," I said.

"I would think she thinks she's better than everybody else," Angel added.

"I would think she'd been playing with her Bedazzler again," Jasmine said, referring to the arts and crafts gun they sell on late-night TV.

"Shut up," Camille snapped.

"All right, Camille," Miss Rachel warned.

"Well, they're the ones picking on me," she said.

"No one is picking on you. If you had been here, you would've known we'd been talking about how it's necessary to look beyond what you see on the outside."

"Yeah, because if we didn't, everyone would think you're a broke-down Beyoncé," Jasmine offered.

"Jasmine, that's enough," Miss Rachel snapped. "Stop antagonizing Camille. You'd be the main one ready to fight if the tables were turned."

"Yeah," Camille echoed.

That seemed to quiet Jasmine.

"Sorry, Camille," Jasmine mumbled.

"It's okay." Camille patted her back. "I know you didn't mean anything."

Jasmine looked at me and whispered, "But her hair is jacked up."

I couldn't help but laugh as Miss Rachel continued talking.

6

Camille

This was a dream come true. I was actually standing on the set of a real live video shoot. People were running back and forth, and the scene looked just like something out of Hollywood. We were filming in this club in the Galleria area. Alexis, Jasmine, Angel and I had come here straight from school. Luckily they let my friends come, because I was nervous as all get out.

"Camille! Looking good, girl," the producer said as she walked my way. Taraji didn't sound genuine, but it was better than the funky attitude she had been giving me the night of the talent show.

"Hi, Taraji," I replied. "I'm so excited about being here." I turned toward my friends. "By the way, these are my frien—"

"So come on, we have to get you in hair and makeup," Taraji cut me off, not giving my friends a second glance. She grabbed my arm and pulled me away. I looked at them helplessly while I tried to keep from stumbling as Taraji tugged on my arm.

"Just one second, okay?" I told her, easing out of her grip. I hurried back over to my friends. "I'm sorry, guys," I whispered.

"Girl, don't sweat it," Alexis replied, waving me off. "This is your day."

I could tell Jasmine was POd by Taraji's rudeness, but judging from the irritated look on Taraji's face, I really didn't have the time to be pacifying her. "Jasmine . . ."

"Camille, time is money, baby," Taraji said before spinning around and walking off.

"Girl, go. She'll be all right," Alexis said, pushing me.

"Yeah, I'm straight," Jasmine finally said. "Go, go, go."

"Okay," I said, breaking out into a big grin. "I'll see you all in a bit." I wished my girls could've come back in the dressing room with me, but Taraji had made it clear that while they could come to the set, they had to stay in a certain area. But they still had a full view of everything, so I'm sure it was all good.

Taraji led me back to something called the green room. There she introduced me to a few people before sitting me down in the makeup chair. She went off to talk to some other people as the two women went to work on me.

It was awesome to have the stylist fussing over my hair while the other woman applied my makeup.

"All right, Camille. Did you have a chance to go over the song?" Taraji asked after she walked back over to me.

"I sure did," I said. I held up the CD she'd delivered the day after I'd told her my mom was going to let me be in the video.

"I know it's short notice, but tell me you have your verse down."

"Oh yeah, my verse and every other verse in the song." I only had a couple of verses, but I had literally stayed up all night practicing that song. It was so tight. After I'd learned my part, I'd learned the whole song. I knew it by heart.

"Good, that's what I like to hear." She clapped her hands together. "Tammy, where's wardrobe?" she asked, looking around the room like she just realized the wardrobe person wasn't there.

"I don't know. She was supposed to be here," the makeup artist replied.

Taraji huffed. "We are on a schedule. Why do you people not get that?"

Before she could continue ranting, the door swung open. A young Asian woman with long blond hair came in holding a bunch of outfits.

"Sorry I'm late," she mumbled. "I just—"

Taraji shot Tammy such a chastising look that Tammy didn't bother finishing her sentence. Taraji snatched the clothes from her and held up a shiny fuchsia minidress. "No," she said, tossing the dress on the floor. "No, no, and no," she said, throwing three more items on the floor. She paused. "Yes." She spun around to face me. "This is perfect."

My mouth fell open at the sight of the skimpy gold skirt. The skirt was super-mini, and it was connected to two wide, suspender-like straps. I took the dress and held the straps up.

"These suspenders are kinda wide, huh?"

Everyone chuckled as Tammy quickly scurried over to me. "No, that's the top of the dress," she said.

"This is a dress?" I asked, my eyes wide.

"The straps crisscross in the front and tie around the neck," Tammy said, demonstrating for me.

I scrunched up my nose in confusion. "What do I wear under this?"

"Nothing, silly," Tammy said, like I was just playing around. "The straps cross over your chest. We'll tape them down."

"Excuse me?" I said. I'm sure the look on my face told her I was dead serious. "I . . . I can't wear that."

"And why not?" Taraji said, turning her attention back on me.

"It's . . . I mean, there's barely anything there," I stammered.

"*And?* Good grief, there's not an ounce of fat on you. Why can't you wear this?" Taraji snapped.

"It . . . it's just so skimpy."

"What did you think you'd be wearing? A turtleneck and a floor-length ruffled skirt?"

"No, but—"

"But nothing. Sam, hurry up with her hair. Mona, that lipstick is too bright. I need Camille on the set in fifteen minutes." Taraji spun and walked out of the room.

I fingered the outfit. There was no way I could wear this. Even if I was bold enough to wear it, my mom would so lose her mind when she saw it.

Mona, the makeup artist, must've read my face. She said, "Girl, just wear the dress, or else they'll think you're difficult. And you don't want to get on Taraji's bad side."

"Yeah," Tammy whispered like Taraji was still in the room. "They got rid of the last girl they called difficult."

Everyone in the room nodded their heads in agreement.

Mona wiped the bright lipstick off my lips. "Just put the dress on, tell yourself it's not as skimpy as it is, and do your thing. Taraji don't play. She will pull you from this video in a minute." She dabbed a darker pink gloss on my lips.

"Maybe I can talk to Sisco," I said after she was done.

"Yeah, if you want to make her even madder," Tammy said.

"For real, the last thing you want to do is go over her head, number one," Mona said. "And number two, if you go in there whining about the outfit, it's not gonna be pretty."

I sighed, knowing they were right. I would have to suck it up, wear the outfit and pray my mom didn't kill me.

Fifteen minutes later, I walked out onto the set. Jasmine, Angel and Alexis were standing around the buffet table nibbling on snacks. Xavier, who had told me he didn't know if he'd be able to get out of basketball practice, was standing next to them.

"Oh, my God," Angel said when I approached them.

"So now you're a video hoochie?" Jasmine asked. They were all staring me up and down.

"Come on, guys," I said, covering myself up with my arms. "I feel self-conscious enough as it is. They're making me wear this."

"Well, at least your body is slamming," Alexis said. Leave it to her to always try to find the positive in a situation.

"Yeah, your body looks good, but does everybody have to see it?" Xavier snapped. His face was clouded with anger. "I mean, I haven't even seen all of this, and now you're getting ready to show it to the whole world?"

Even though his basketball teammates had been giving him a hard time, Xavier and I hadn't slept together. He respected my decision to wait and never pressured me to do anything I didn't want to. So I could understand his anger at seeing his girlfriend half-clothed.

"Are you for real? I mean, really, Camille?" he asked again as he continued to take in my outfit.

"Babe," I pleaded with him, "they're making me wear it."

"Camille," Taraji called from across the room.

"I gotta go," I said sheepishly. I needed Xavier to be with me on this, but judging from the look on his face, that wasn't happening. I made my way back over to the set.

"Dang, girl, I didn't know you had it going on like that," Sisco said as I walked up.

One of the cameramen whistled and I felt so—I don't know—cheap.

Seeing my expression, Sisco asked, "What's the matter?" He was sitting on the edge of one of the props, drinking a Red Bull as some man tried to adjust the lighting over his head.

I shrugged, glancing back toward Taraji, who was standing right behind me. "I'm okay."

"She's fine," Taraji said. "She's a professional, not some little high school girl."

"No, I can tell something's wrong." Sisco noticed me covering myself. "Oh snap, you all self-conscious?"

I covered myself tighter. "Well . . . this dress. It's kinda revealing. I'm a little classier than this."

"You don't like the outfit? Why didn't you say so?" He turned back to Taraji. "Get baby girl something else to wear."

"What?" she snapped.

"I said, find her something else," he said casually.

"Sisco, we don't have time for this," Taraji protested. "The director is on a tight schedule."

"Come on, Taraji. If the girl ain't comfortable, she's not gonna do her best, and I need her game to be tight."

Taraji gritted her teeth and shot me an evil look, which Sisco noticed right away.

"And don't start trippin' with her. She didn't ask me to change it. I could just tell she was uncomfortable."

Taraji groaned and rolled her eyes. "Fine. Come on," she said, stomping off. "This is exactly why I didn't want to fool with these stupid high school girls," she muttered.

Mona's words rang in my head, and I knew I was now on Taraji's bad side.

7

Alexis

I couldn't tell everything that was going on, but judging from the way Camille was covering herself and the scowl on that Taraji lady's face, I could tell it wasn't good.

When Camille emerged from the dressing room ten minutes later, she looked a whole lot better. Granted, the dress she had changed into was still short, but it wasn't so hoochie. It was a short-sleeve royal blue silk number that hung off one shoulder. A rope belt was tied around the waist, and the back was cut low and dipped down to the small of her back, stopping at the top of her behind. But at least the front was covered.

I gave Camille a thumbs-up and mouthed "Much better." I nudged Jasmine, who gave her a smile as well. Camille seemed to relax as she made her way back over to Sisco.

"Is that better?" Sisco asked her.

"Much," Camille replied with a smile.

"Do you need anything else, Princess Camille?" Taraji snapped.

"No, I'm fine," Camille said.

"Then do you think we can get started now?"

Camille took a deep breath. I hoped she wasn't letting that Taraji woman get to her. This was her time to shine, and I wanted her to be on top of her game.

Camille loosened up when Sisco took her hand and led her onto the set. I glanced over at Xavier. Maybe his being here wasn't such a good idea, because he stood with his lips awfully tight. I could tell it was taking everything in his power not to get upset.

Jasmine must've noticed it too, because she looked at me and nodded. Angel was too giddy to notice a thing.

The music started up, bringing our attention back to the set. Camille was in place, and honestly, she looked like she was born for this.

The song was a slow, up-tempo melody called "Just One More Chance." I could tell right away that it was going to be a hit.

Sisco finished up his solo part, then turned to Camille, who was doing a sexy strut like she was just passing in front of him. Sisco sang something about being sorry, and Camille, with attitude in full force, sang back, asking why she should give him another chance.

Angel clutched my arm, trying to contain her excitement. She was doing what I call a quiet scream.

"Girl, chill," I whispered.

"Okay, okay," she said. "I'm just so proud of her."

"She is doing good," Jasmine said, nodding with a big smile across her face.

Someone standing in front of us holding a clipboard turned around and hissed, "Ssshhhh."

We all covered our mouths and continued watching Camille. Sisco sang some more before Camille finally decided to go ahead and give him a chance. When she sang about "loving her right or not loving her at all," I thought I was going to cry. My girl nailed it.

Sisco closed up the song promising to love her forever as he leaned in close. He was a good actor, because he sure looked like he was about to plant a deep kiss on her. I was expecting the director to yell "cut" at any moment. My eyes suddenly grew wide when their lips met. He pulled her close and kissed her as the music died down. I don't know if Camille had known the kiss was coming—she sure hadn't said anything to us about it—but she didn't miss a beat as she got into the kiss.

Only when Sisco pulled away from Camille did I see the stunned look on her face. "Can your man kiss you like that?" Sisco said, smiling mischievously.

Before Camille could respond, Xavier rushed toward the set. The grin left Sisco's face as Xavier tackled him to the floor. "Xavier!" Camille screamed.

Total chaos broke out. Two big, burly guys came out of nowhere. They jumped on Xavier and pinned him on the floor. Sisco was screaming and cursing as he struggled to get up. Taraji was yelling that this was exactly why she "wanted to keep the set closed." And my heart dropped when I noticed tears streaming down Camille's face.

Jasmine and Angel must've known exactly what I was thinking, because we all raced to Camille's side.

"Please don't hurt him," she cried when Sisco kicked Xavier in the side.

"Who is this boy, and why is he attacking my artist?" the director bellowed.

"He's my boyfriend," Camille whimpered. "I don't know what happened."

"Get him out of here before I catch a case," Sisco snapped, trying to calm himself down.

Xavier was still struggling, although it wasn't doing him any good. The big bodyguard had Xavier's arms pinned behind his back.

They pulled him up, then dragged him out toward the back. Camille immediately began to follow him.

"And just where do you think you're going?" Taraji hissed.

"I . . . I need to go check on my—on Xavier," she sniffed.

"Little girl, you have been more trouble than you're worth." Taraji stepped closer. "Right about now, the only person you need to be trying to pacify is Sisco, because I guarantee you, you don't want to make him mad. If you go after that thug, you can forget about this video."

Camille paused and looked helplessly at us. I knew she wanted to go after Xavier, but I understood her dilemma.

"Look, we'll go check on Xavier," Jasmine said, stepping forward. "You just go handle your business."

"If I were you, I'd listen to your friends," Taraji said before stomping off.

"Seriously," I said. "We'll go after Xavier, make sure he calms down. That lady is right. Sisco is not going to like getting embarrassed like that, so you might need to go smooth that over."

Camille glanced over at Sisco, who was pacing back and

forth, his hands clenched. Several people were trying to calm him down.

"Go on, we got your back," Angel said.

Camille took a deep breath. "Okay, thank you so much. Please tell Xavier I didn't know he was gonna kiss me. I'll call you guys later, okay?"

We all gave her a quick hug. I only hoped that she could get through to Sisco, because Xavier might've just ruined her one chance at stardom.

8

Alexis

$\mathcal{I}$ was so sick of what had become a normal day in my household.

"I said I don't want to talk about it anymore," my dad screamed right before I heard a door slam.

"Fine!" I heard my mother say as another door slammed.

I was on the phone with Camille, lying on my bed listening to the daily ritual of my parents fighting. Camille was talking about her hair, of all things. I was finding it hard to concentrate on what she was saying while the commotion was going on in the other room.

"Earth to Alexis! Hel-lo! Are you even listening to me? I was trying to ask for your advice about what to do," Camille whined on the other end of the phone.

I shook off the tears building behind my eyelids. "I'm sorry, girl, my parents are at it again, and it's driving me crazy. I just don't know what to do at this point."

I was about to tell Camille what was going on at my house, but as usual, she quickly turned the conversation back to her.

"Girl, your parents will work it out, but what should I do? The stylist said my hair needs to be spiced up. She thought I should go honey brown like Tyra Banks. Come to think of it, all the stars have that blondish, honey brown flavor— Beyoncé, Christina Milian. So maybe that is the way to go."

I was too through. She'd been talking about her hair for the past thirty minutes. She'd gotten rid of that crazy weave and was trying to figure out what else to do.

Right about now, though, Camille's hair was the least of my problems. I had drama of my own that she obviously didn't seem to care about.

"So what do you think?" she asked again.

"I think I'm getting off the phone."

I hung up on Camille before she could say another word. My head was buzzing as I lay back on my bed and thought about the fighting going on between my parents.

The house was eerily quiet. My dad must have stormed out into the night. It wasn't the first time that had happened. I could hear my mom walking down the hall on her way past my room. I heard her sniffling, which concerned me a lot more than the usual dramatic, fit-for-Hollywood crying spells that she usually had.

I jumped off the bed and flung open my door. "Mom, are you okay?"

I was a little shocked at my mother's appearance. Her hair

was smashed to one side of her face, and her eyes were red and puffy. I could tell she had been crying a while.

She pulled her robe tighter and looked at me with sad eyes. "I'm okay, Lexi."

As I looked at her, the tears I'd been fighting back found their way out. This was not the woman I knew as my mom. That woman was always confident, poised, and well put together. She would never let anyone disrespect her, and she definitely didn't get upset and cry because things weren't going her way. She just found a way to make them work how she wanted them to work. It broke my heart to see her so defeated.

"Mom, I can tell you've been crying. I know we've grown apart over the past few years, but I am still your daughter," I said, easing toward her. "Plus, I hear you and Dad arguing all the time. I'm not a little girl anymore. I know what's going on."

My mom took a deep breath. "Lexi, don't worry about it. This is between your dad and me. You're too young to understand."

"Actually, no, I'm not," I replied firmly. "I'm seventeen years old, so I am well aware of what's going on. I'm not a kid anymore, and I deserve to know what's happening in my own family."

"Sweetheart, I can't deal with this right now," she said, turning to walk away from me.

"Are you and Dad getting a divorce?"

The question stopped her in her tracks. She was silent for too long. Now I wasn't sure I was ready to hear the answer.

She turned back around to face me. "To be honest with you, baby, it is an option," she said tearfully. She walked me into my room, and we sat down on my bed.

"I don't want you to worry, but your dad and I have talked about it. You know that things have not been good for a long time, but we are trying to work through our problems. We both know how hard a divorce would be on you and your . . ." She let her words trail off. My mom always had a hard time talking about my sister. "Well, tomorrow, when your dad is home, the three of us will all sit down and talk about some things. But for now, I want you to try to get some sleep and try not to worry."

"I could say the same thing to you," I said softly. I was trying to wrap my mind around the fact that my parents might actually be divorcing. No, I told myself, that's not what they wanted to talk about. I convinced myself that they wanted to apologize for the way things had been and talk about how we could all make it right.

My mom kissed me on my forehead. "I'll try to sleep if you will," she promised. She attempted a smile as she backed out of my room.

I lay back down on my bed and contemplated calling one of my girls. As I reached for the phone, though, I changed my mind. Jasmine couldn't talk on the phone this late. Angel was probably putting Angelica to sleep, and Camille was too caught up in her own drama to worry about mine. I looked at my bedroom window, hoping to see headlights that would tell me my father had decided to turn around and come back home. I watched for a long time, but it stayed dark. I had never felt so all alone.

9

Camille

Today we were going to be shooting the last part of the video over, because Sisco hadn't wanted to do anything after yesterday's disaster with Xavier. The director had said we'd just start fresh today.

I was so glad my girls decided to come, though for some reason Alexis didn't seem her usual self. I was still a little bummed out. Xavier had broken up with me by text. I'd tried to call him, but he'd slammed the phone down in my face. Normally, I would've called him back and gone off, but I was going to give him a pass, since I knew he was pretty upset about Sisco kissing me.

Speaking of the kiss, I'd been thinking about it all night long. Yeah, I knew it was all part of Sisco's act, but if this time a month ago someone had told me I'd be kissing Sisco, I'd have thought they were crazy.

"Are you all right?" Angel asked. We'd just made our way into the parking lot. I'd been pretty much quiet the whole way over here.

"I'm okay. I just hope me and Xavier can get through this, because he's a good guy."

"He is," Angel added. "And he'll get over the whole kissing thing."

"I don't know," Jasmine said doubtfully. Alexis and Angel shot her the evil eye, and she turned her lip up.

"All I know is when everything is said and done, Xavier is the one who will be there for you," Jasmine retorted. "Sisco will be gone on to his next video vixen. So don't kick Xavier to the curb."

"I am not a video vixen," I protested.

"I'm just saying, Sisco has a million girls throwing themselves at him."

"I'm not throwing myself at him," I snapped. "I'm not dumping Xavier for Sisco. He quit me, remember?"

"It's not your fault that Sisco kissed you," Angel said helpfully.

"I know," I replied, getting frustrated all over again.

"But it is her fault that she had her tongue down his throat as much as he was slobbing all over her," Jasmine said.

"Shut up, Jasmine. I did not have my tongue down his throat. It was just a regular old kiss."

"Umph, I ain't never had a regular old kiss like that," Jasmine giggled.

Alexis broke in. "Okay, Jaz, don't make it any worse. You know Camille feels bad as it is."

"All right, all right. I'm sorry. I was just messing with you." Jasmine threw up her hands apologetically. "But seriously, don't sweat it. Yeah, Xavier is mad, but he'll get over it. Right now you're about to blow up, and you can't let some jealous boyfriend ruin that for you."

I sighed and leaned back. Jasmine was right. My mind drifted back to the chemistry that Sisco and I had in the video shoot. I couldn't deny it, we looked good together. And although the kiss had caught me off guard, it had been nice.

I finally got a hold of my thoughts. This was all an act. It's not like me and Sisco ever stood a chance of being together in real life.

"We're here," Alexis said, pulling into a parking spot.

We were giggling and laughing as we approached the security guard.

"Hi, I'm Camille Harris," I said.

"Hey," the tall, muscular guy said as he stepped back to let me pass. "You don't have to introduce yourself to me, baby girl. I saw you yesterday. You're the next big star."

I smiled as I led the way in. But as soon as I turned to walk off, I heard Jasmine say, "Excuse me?"

I looked back to see that the guard had stepped in front of Jasmine, Angel and Alexis, blocking their path.

"Oh, they're with me," I said.

"Okay," he said, without moving.

"Okay, then move," Jasmine snapped.

"I'm not goin' to be able to do that, little lady." He crossed his stocky arms across his chest.

"What? We were here yesterday," Alexis said.

"And I hope you enjoyed it," he replied.

"There must be some kind of mistake," I said, walking

back up to the security guard. "These are my friends, and they're here with me."

"They're not getting in," he said with finality. Before I could say anything, I saw Taraji strutting toward us.

"Taraji, I'm so glad you're here," I said. "He won't let my friends in."

"I know," she responded sharply. "Come on, you need to go get dressed. Thanks to your boyfriend's attack yesterday, Sisco isn't in the mood to shoot, so we're just going to shoot some promotional stuff. Let's go." She kept walking.

"Taraji!" I called after her. "What's going on? Why can't my friends come in?"

She spun around like she was irritated that she even had to explain anything to me. "Look here, girl, you're lucky that we're even letting you come back after that disaster with your boyfriend. I can't tell you the last time I saw Sisco that mad. So, sorry, but there's no room for your friends. The set is closed."

My mouth dropped open. "You mean they can't come in?"

"What part of no don't you get, the *n* or the *o*?"

"But—"

"But you're late. And you're hanging on by a thread yourself. If I were you, I'd tell your little friends good-bye and get to the dressing room."

"Camille, go on," Alexis said. "We'll be fine."

"No, we won't," Jasmine snapped. "We didn't do anything."

I felt so bad as I pleadingly looked at Taraji.

"I do not have time to stand out here and debate with some ghetto high school girls."

"Ghetto? You want me to show you what we do in the ghetto?" Jasmine asked, taking a step forward.

Thank God Alexis stepped up and stopped her. "For real, Camille, you go on. We'll catch up with you later."

"Listen to your friends," Taraji told me nonchalantly. "Or better yet, why don't you just go with them?" She spun off and walked away before I could respond.

"Are you guys sure about me going on?" I asked.

"We're fine," Angel said. "And it's not like you have a lot of choices."

"Jasmine?"

"I'm all right," she said, waving me off. The attitude was still evident all over her face, but I knew she wasn't mad at me. Jasmine worked real hard to keep her temper at bay, so she probably was upset that she'd let Taraji get to her.

"Do you need me to come back and pick you up?" Alexis asked.

"Nah, I'll just call my mom," I said, suddenly wishing I had the money to get my old car fixed. It hadn't worked in about a year. I was definitely going to see if my mom would let me buy a car with the money I made from the video shoot.

"Okay, just call us later," Angel said. Jasmine had already turned and started heading toward the car.

"I'm sorry," I mumbled again before taking off inside.

10

Alexis

"Hey, baby mama."

I busted out laughing at the sight of Miss Rachel's twelve-year-old wannabe pimp daddy son, Jordan. He was standing outside the Good Girlz meeting room. He was tall for his age, but he still had a baby face, with deep dimples. He wore his school uniform top with some khaki pants.

"Hey, baby mama," he repeated when Jasmine didn't respond. Jordan's little behind was always flirting with Jasmine. He was adorable, but he was *twelve*. So the sight of him trying to play a mack daddy was hilarious.

"When are you going to stop playing hard to get and give me a shot?" he slyly said.

I laughed even harder when I saw Miss Rachel come up behind him. I knew what was coming next.

"Owwww!" he yelled when she popped him upside the back of his head.

"Boy, what are you talking about, 'baby mama'? I don't know why y'all think there's something cute about that term. Ain't nothing cute about being a baby mama."

"You got that right," Angel muttered.

Miss Rachel should know about the struggles of a young mother. She'd had her first child at fifteen and her second two years later. She had shared with us how she'd been through a lot before she'd grown up, at least mentally. So she was adamant about us learning from her mistakes.

"Mama, you trippin'," Jordan said, rubbing the back of his head.

"I've also told you about talking to me like I'm one of your little friends," she responded sternly.

"Dang, Mama. Chill. Can you please not embarrass me in front of my future wife?" He grinned widely and winked at Jasmine.

We all busted out laughing again as Miss Rachel swatted him once more.

"Boy, get your little mannish behind in the church with your father. And where's your sister?"

"She's in the office with Daddy Lester."

"Well, go in there with them and I will see you all at home. And make sure you do your homework."

"Why can't I be in the Good Girlz?" he asked, heading to the door. "I could be your first male member, or an honorary member."

"Jordan Kobe Clark, if you don't get your tail in there with your father . . ."

"A'ight, a'ight," he said. "Bye, baby," he said to Jasmine.

"Oh, Jasmine is the only one you see?" I joked.

"Awww, Alexis, you know I got love for you, but it ain't even like that. You're too light-skinned for me."

I gasped. Not like I would ever want him, but still . . .

"Now, Angel, yo quiero Taco Bell," he sang, scurrying out of the door before his mother swatted him again.

"Did he just ask me if I wanted some Taco Bell?" Angel asked, confused.

"It's the only Spanish he knows," Miss Rachel said. "I've told you all, don't pay that little boy any attention."

"Well, you've got your hands full, Miss Rachel," I said, "because if he's like this at twelve, I can only imagine what he'll be like at fifteen and sixteen."

"Don't remind me," Miss Rachel groaned as she set her Bible on the front table.

We walked into the room and got settled.

"Where is Camille?" she asked, noticing just the three of us.

"Where is she always?" Jasmine snidely remarked. "Off playing superstar."

I know Jasmine was still mad about them not letting us on the set yesterday, but Camille hadn't bothered to call us afterward. Then today at lunch she blew us off when Sisco called.

"I think they had to reshoot the video today," I said.

"I hope she doesn't just throw us to the side," Rachel said. "I'm very proud of the progress you girls have made, and I would hate for Camille to forget all of that."

"Tell me about it." Jasmine was about to say something else when a girl standing in the doorway caught our eye.

Rachel smiled, then motioned for the girl to come in the room.

She wore a cute Baby Phat T-shirt and some skinny jeans. She had braces with pink rubber bands around them. Other than the cheesy rubber bands, she actually was very cute.

"Ladies," Rachel began, "this is Tyeesha McCray."

We all stared, too surprised to speak.

"What's your name again?" Jasmine finally said.

"Tyeesha," the girl repeated, like she was used to being asked that question.

We all looked at each other and tried our best not to break out laughing.

"You got a problem?" Tyeesha said, her hands planted firmly on her hips.

"No problem at all," I said, trying to keep a straight face.

"Girls, that is very rude," Rachel said. "Come on in, Tyee-sha, and have a seat."

"I thought you said this group was all about being open and honest. So I wanna know what they found so funny."

"They don't find anything funny. Do you, girls?" Rachel asked.

"Actually," Jasmine giggled, "we're just trippin' off your name."

"Jasmine," Rachel immediately chastised.

"What, you've never seen a white girl named Tyeesha?" the girl said.

"Nope," all three of us said at the same time.

"Well, we do not discriminate based on color, religion, or name, Jasminium Nichelle Solé Jones," Rachel said. That wiped the smile off Jasmine's face. She hated her full name with a passion.

"Now, *that's* funny," Tyeesha said. She flashed a wide grin, displaying her pink braces again. "So I'm here, Miss Rachel. You claim this group is what I need. So let's see." She strolled into the room and took a seat next to Angel.

Normally, her brazenness would've been a turnoff, but there was something about this girl that I liked. She had a lot of spunk, and that told me she was going to be a lot of fun.

"Okay, girls, because we have a new member to the Good Girlz Club, we'll start by having her introduce herself. Then each of you will do the same and tell her what you've gotten out of the Good Girlz." She gave a warm smile. "Tyeesha?"

Tyeesha cleared her throat as she stood up. "Well, you know my name," she said, flashing her big grin again. "And let the record reflect, I'm proud of my name and my race."

"Hey, I ain't mad at you," I told her.

"Yeah, we don't have a problem with your race," Angel said dismissively. "Alexis is half white."

"My mother is biracial," I corrected. "I'm multiracial."

"Okay, Tiger Woods," Jasmine laughed.

"Anyway," Tyeesha continued, "I was forced to come to the Good Girlz"—she eyed Rachel—"after getting in a little vandalizing trouble with this group of kids I was hanging out with."

"Vandalizing?" I asked. "What did you vandalize?"

She looked uneasily to Miss Rachel.

"Go ahead," Rachel said encouragingly.

Tyeesha paused, then said, "Okay, I vandalized a church."

"A church?" we all exclaimed.

She sighed. "This church."

"What? You're the one who wrote all over the side of Zion Hill?" I asked. A few months ago, we'd arrived at our Good

Girlz meeting to find that someone had covered the back of the church in graffiti. They hadn't sprayed anything derogatory, just some fancy names, but it still was messed up. Plus, they'd thrown rocks through two back windows.

We all had done our share of things we weren't too proud of, but to vandalize a church?

"Yeah, I know, it was a stupid thing to do. But I took a dare from the people I was hanging out with." Tyeesha looked genuinely remorseful.

"Wow," I said.

"Tyeesha and her friends didn't know about our video cameras, so it wasn't too hard to catch them," Rachel put in.

"Yeah," Tyeesha continued. "My friends got in major trouble, but since it was my first offense, Miss Rachel asked the people here to agree not to press charges if I came to the Good Girlz, so here I am."

"So where do you go to school?"

"Nimitz, but I'll be starting at Madison next week."

"You're going to our school?" Angel asked.

"Yep, starting Monday. My parents are getting a divorce, so me and my mom had to move in with my grandmother."

That caused my ears to perk up. "Divorce? Dang, sorry to hear that."

She tossed her hand in the air. "Whatever. I'm glad they finally got a divorce, because them living together and all their fighting was about to drive me crazy."

I knew there was a reason I liked this girl. I could definitely relate to everything she was saying. I had a feeling that Tyeesha and I would find out we had a whole lot in common.

II

Camille

I was in my dressing room, waiting for the video shoot to start, when I thought of Xavier. I dialed star 67 to block my number, then punched in his cell phone number.

He answered on the second ring. "Hello."

I hesitated, then said, "Hey, Xavier."

He was silent for a moment before his voice took on a firm tone. "What do you want?"

"I just wanted to check on you and see how you were doing."

"For what?" From the sound of his voice I could tell that he was trying to act like he wasn't fazed about anything, but I knew better.

I sighed. "Xavier, how long are you going to stay mad at me?"

"I'm not mad at you," he said. "You do you. It's all good."

"Xavier, you are trippin'," I snapped.

He blew a deep breath before saying, "Camille, I'm not even about to go there with you."

I decided to try a different approach. "I just don't want us to be done," I said softly. "I mean, can we at least talk about this?" When I'd dialed, I hadn't planned on begging him. On the real, I don't beg for any boy to be with me, but something about hearing his voice got me all emotional. Besides, I knew he was upset. Xavier really liked me. We started going together after he was assigned as my science lab partner. Out of all the boyfriends I'd ever had, he definitely was the best. Even though he was a jock, he was smart, cute and respectful.

Silence briefly filled the phone. "Are you still doing the video?" he finally asked.

I took a deep breath. "Yes, but—"

"Then it's nothing else for us to talk about," he said, cutting me off.

"Let me ask you a question," I said, preparing the speech I had practiced last night. "Do you think Jay-Z has a problem with Beyoncé dancing all provocatively and kissing dudes in her video? No, he doesn't. He understands that it's acting. That's what we do."

He busted out laughing.

"What's so funny?" I asked.

"First of all," he said, trying to hold back his laughter, "you ain't and you never will be a Beyoncé. So I don't know what all this 'we' stuff is."

I sat up straight in my chair, trying to make sure I'd heard him correctly. "What do you mean? You don't think I'm talented?"

"I mean, yeah, you can dance, and even blow, but Beyoncé? Get real." He laughed again. "You couldn't even be a backup for Beyoncé."

Now he was really making me mad. "Well, Sisco seems to think I'm talented enough," I said. I hadn't planned on going there, but if he wanted to trip with me, I could trip right back.

He suddenly stopped laughing and didn't say anything. I smiled, knowing I'd made him mad.

"What, you ain't got nothing to say now?" I decided to keep laying it on. I'd sucked up my pride and called him, and he wanted to throw salt in my game? I don't think so. "In fact, truth be told, Sisco says I'm cuter, finer, and I even sound better than Beyoncé."

I waited for his comeback, but instead all I heard was the sound of a phone slamming down in my face.

"Ugggh!" I screamed, tossing my cell onto the makeup table. "He makes me sick!" I screamed.

"Girl, who makes you sick?" asked this long-legged girl in Daisy Duke shorts, a cropped tank top and a long, curly weave cascading down her back. She was standing in the doorway of the dressing room.

"Oh, I'm sorry," I said, standing up. "I didn't mean to be so loud."

The girl walked into the room. She looked like she was in her early twenties. When she came closer, I recognized her as one of the dancers from the video.

"Girl, please," she said, leaning over and checking her lipstick in the mirror. "Sounds to me like you got man drama." Satisfied with her lipstick, she turned to me. "I'm Maya."

"You're one of the dancers, right? Sorry I didn't realize it right away."

She shrugged. "That's all right. I'm in the background, so everybody don't recognize me." She fluffed her hair. "But that's 'bout to change. I'm about to make a name for myself in the video game." She looked me up and down. "I heard you out there. You got skills."

I sighed heavily. "Not to let my boyfriend tell it."

"That buster that jumped on Sisco?" she asked.

I nodded.

She waved her hand. "Girl, please. You don't need to be fooling with him anyway. You're major now. And see, regular dudes, they can't handle when their girl becomes a star. And you are definitely on your way to being a star. Along with me," she added.

I immediately liked her. Even though she was dressed like a hoochie mama, she made me feel better with just those few remarks.

"Anyway," she said as she took my arm, "you need to start hanging with me and my girls. We'll introduce you to the kind of guys you need to be dealing with."

"I'm not trying to find a guy," I countered. I definitely didn't want her to think I was all about hooking up with celebrities. "I'm just lovin' being in this video with Sisco."

"Sweetheart, this is just the beginning. By the time this video hits the air, you won't have to find a guy. They'll find you," she said, leading me out of the room.

I made my way onto the set. Sisco was already there,

going over some notes. "Hey, baby girl," he said, looking up. I was grateful to see he didn't look mad anymore.

"Hey."

"You good?" He motioned toward my black catsuit.

"I'm good," I replied. The outfit was skintight, but it wasn't revealing, so I really couldn't complain.

"You got your boy in check? Because I would sure hate to check him myself." He was trying to look all tough, even though he'd shown nothing tough the other day when Xavier had bum-rushed him.

"No, you don't have to worry about him," I said, suddenly feeling sad about our fight.

Sisco pinched my chin, a sexy smile crossing his lips. "Truth be told, I ain't even mad at him. If I had a chick as fine as you, I'd probably be protective, too."

That made me blush. "You tight, girl." He looked me up and down, nodding his approval. "Real tight, with mad skills."

I kept blushing. This is what I was talking about. At least someone appreciated my talents.

"All right. Places, everyone," the director said.

We started from the top, and I ignored all the eyes that were on me as the music thumped throughout the building. I imagined that I really was Sisco's jilted girlfriend and that he was begging me for another chance.

I sang my part about taking him back. I threw my arms around him, as the script called for. He had just finished singing, and he was coming in for the part where we were supposed to kiss. I tried to relax. Even though none of my friends were on the set, I knew everyone and their mama would see the video.

But then I thought about Xavier tripping. So I pushed everything out of my mind and kissed Sisco back, long and hard as he pulled me closer. That part I could deal with, but then he lifted my leg, ran his hand up my thigh and squeezed my behind. I wanted to push him away, but I was too shocked, not to mention scared of causing any more drama.

"And cut!" I heard Mark, the director, yell as the music faded. "Love it, love it, love it! Boy, I tell you the chemistry between you two is great." He looked so thrilled.

"Man, that is on fire," someone standing next to him said.

I faked a smile as several more people came over to congratulate us, but when I found myself alone with Sisco, I had to say something.

"Hey, umm, what's with you feeling all over me?" Don't get me wrong, I'm no prude, but I couldn't appreciate some dude feeling me up. Even if that dude was a superstar.

Sisco flashed a lopsided smile. "That's what they call ad-libbing, babe. Shoot, the way you was kissing me, you can't tell me you didn't like it."

"Actually, no. It was a bit much," I said nervously.

The smile left his face. "Oh, you worried about ol' boy?"

I nodded. I actually wasn't thinking as much about Xavier as I was about my mom totally blowing a gasket. But I definitely didn't want to tell him that.

"Okay." He sighed in defeat. "It's no biggie. I'll just tell Mark to have the editors take it out. They shoot a bunch of different shots, so it shouldn't be a problem."

"Thank you so much, Sisco," I said gratefully.

"I told you it's no problem, babe. Holla at you later."

I felt so relieved as I watched him walk away. He really was one of the good guys.

12

Camille

I had just left the pizza line in the cafeteria when I heard someone say, "Hey, Camille, you wanna come sit with us?"

I turned to see Dee. She was president of the Theta Ladies, a high school sorority that I had so wanted to join at one time. But that had turned into a nightmare because of Tori, the girl who'd been president at the time. She had tried to keep Angel out of the organization because of the color of her skin, and the situation had turned messy. She'd graduated last year, but the whole experience had left a sour taste in my mouth for the Thetas.

"Thanks, Dee, but I'm supposed to be meeting Jasmine and Angel," I lied. Every time I'd even tried to talk to my friends over the past two days, someone from Sisco's camp would call and interrupt us. I knew they would start tripping about how busy I was, so the last thing I wanted to be doing was sitting up and faking the funk with Dee and her friends, especially because I knew the only reason they wanted me over there was because of everything that was going on with Sisco. Thanks, but no thanks.

"Whatever," I heard this girl named Veronica mumble when I walked off. "She thinks she's all that just 'cause she's in a stupid video."

I smiled to myself. Let the hate begin.

I glanced around the cafeteria, trying to find my girls. They usually sat in the back, so that's where I headed. I stopped in my tracks when I spotted them. Jasmine, Alexis, Angel, Xavier and two of his friends were sitting at the table laughing with some girl I'd never seen. My problem was the way Xavier was leaning over the new girl, looking at her like she was a tasty pork chop.

I eased closer to the table. "Hey," I said meekly.

The laughing stopped as everyone looked at me. Alexis was the first to speak. "Hey, Camille. Where you been?"

"Where you think?" Jasmine snapped. "With her A-list friends. Alexis, didn't you get the memo? You're C-list. You can only hang out with Camille on the third Sunday of the month."

I rolled my eyes. "Whatever, Jasmine."

She must've noticed the strange look on my face, because she stopped laughing. "Girl, I'm just playing."

I didn't respond. "Hey, Xavier."

He pushed off from the table. "And on that note, Gerald, Smitty, let's roll," he said to his friends.

I set my tray down next to Angel. I couldn't believe he was

being such a jerk. I mean, I know we broke up, but he didn't have to act so stank.

"Jaz, don't forget I need to copy your calculus homework," Xavier said as his friends stood up. He turned to the new girl. "Tyeesha, it was nice to meet you. I sure hope to see you around."

Tyeesha laughed. "I'll be here. And it was nice to meet you, too."

I wanted to cringe as Xavier squeezed her shoulder. He walked past me without uttering a word. Gerald and Smitty tried to fight back laughs as they followed behind him.

My emotions were all mixed up. On the one hand, I wanted to cry. On the other, I was ready to go off. I took a deep breath. The last thing I needed to be getting into was some drama, so I just let it slide. If Xavier wanted to be a prick, then fine.

I looked over at Jasmine, Alexis and Angel, who had suddenly grown interested in their lunch trays. I was about to say something when it dawned on me that the new girl was still sitting there. "Ummm, do you mind?"

She popped the last of her pizza in her mouth and shrugged. "Not at all." She took a long swig of her soda.

I tapped my tray impatiently. "No, I mean, that's my seat."

Tyeesha (don't even get me started on her name) looked confused. Then she stood up, looked at the seat, under the seat and on the table. "I'm sorry, somebody must've taken your name plate off of here. You might want to take that up with your publicist." She smiled, then sat back down.

Jasmine busted out laughing. "Okay, see, this is why I like this girl."

Me, on the other hand, I didn't see anything funny.

"Look, Tyequanna, Myesha, whatever your name is, I really need to talk to my girls."

"Okay, so talk," she said.

"Alone."

"We're all family now, so you might as well get to talking." Tyeesha flashed a tight smile.

"What?" I wasn't in the mood to deal with this girl. "Who are you and what are you talking about?"

"I'm Tyeesha McCray," she said, all friendly-like. "And I'm good, girl."

It was my turn to look confused. "What do you mean, you're good?"

"Ummm," Angel said hesitantly, "just what she said."

Jasmine finally stopped snickering. "Oh, good grief. Camille, meet Tyeesha, our newest Good Girl."

I'm surprised that I didn't faint right then and there. "Excuse me?"

Jasmine spun around on her stool. "If you had time to come to a Good Girlz meeting, you'd know she was a new member."

"Since when did we start getting new members? And more importantly, why didn't you guys tell her Xavier is my boyfriend?"

"Dang, X-man is your boyfriend?" Tyeesha asked, wide-eyed.

"Technically, *X-man* is her *ex,*" Jasmine snickered.

Angel shoved her in the side. I knew Jasmine was just messing with me, but I wasn't in the mood. "Who the heck is X-man?" I snapped.

That made Angel and Jasmine giggle even more. At least Alexis had the decency not to be laughing at my misery.

"Chill out, Camille," Alexis said. "We were going to tell her Xavier is off limits, but he'd just sat down before you got here."

"Yeah, chill, Camille," Tyeesha said. "We're BFFs now. I wouldn't dare talk to your man . . . no matter how much he tried," she added with a smirk.

I glared at her. Good Girl or not, she would never be my friend. And right about now, I was beginning to question the ones I did call my friends. "Whatever," I said, stomping off.

I ignored my friends as they called my name. I had suddenly lost my appetite.

13

Alexis

I normally had to be the voice of reason among my friends. Angel never caused any drama, but she was quiet and tried to stay neutral, so the peacemaker role fell to me. I could tell I was definitely going to have to play it today.

Camille had walked into the Good Girlz meeting without speaking to anyone. After everything that had gone down at school today, I honestly was surprised to even see Camille here. But judging from her sequined tank top, low-cut skinny jeans and high-heeled boots, I couldn't help but wonder if she was going to an awards show when she left the meeting.

"Well, hello, Camille," Rachel said. "So nice of you to join us."

"Hey," was all she said.

Rachel eyed her funny, then looked at us. I kinda shrugged. Tyeesha had a nervous smile.

"Okay, does someone want to tell me what's going on?" Rachel said. When no one responded, she continued, "Camille?"

"Nothing," Camille replied nonchalantly, removing her sunglasses.

Rachel set her pen down, folded her arms and walked around to the front of her table. "I'm going to ask again. Does someone want to tell me what's going on?"

"Ask Tyeesha what the problem is," Camille snapped.

"What did I do?" Tyeesha responded.

"You're trying to steal my man."

"First of all, he's not your man anymore. Second of all, I didn't try to steal him. I didn't flirt with him. I was just laughing at something he said. But now that I know you two used to date I won't even do that."

"See, Camille," Angel interjected, trying to smooth things over. "It's not that serious. Tyeesha's cool, don't be upset with her."

Camille cut her eyes but didn't respond.

"You haven't been here," Jasmine said nonchalantly.

"I haven't been here because of the video. I thought you guys understood that. In fact, you were the ones encouraging me. Now you want to punish me for it."

"Okay, here comes Camille the victim," Jasmine groaned.

"Okay, girls. Enough," Rachel said.

"No, Miss Rachel," Camille said. "It's not fair. They were the main ones encouraging me."

"Camille, I think they just want you to find a balance," Rachel said gently.

"Yeah, Camille, find balance," Jasmine sneered.

Miss Rachel cut her eyes. "That's the last time, Jasmine."

She shrugged apologetically.

"Camille, you can accomplish great things without stepping on anyone to get there," Miss Rachel continued. "Remember that the same people you step on on your way up are the same people that you will see on your way down."

"I'm not stepping on anyone," Camille cried.

Miss Rachel sighed heavily. "You know what? I have to run into my office and make a call. I want you all to discuss this like the mature young ladies that you are. And I'm confident that when I return, you all will have resolved this on your own."

She left, and we sat in silence before Tyeesha finally spoke up. "Okay, since I'm new, let me play mediator."

Camille turned up her top lip, but Tyeesha didn't let Camille faze her. "Okay, Jasmine, we'll start with you. What's your problem with Camille?"

Jasmine used her hand to flick the question off, but Tyeesha was persistent. "Come on, y'all. Miss Rachel is expecting us to have worked this out. Let's show her that we are indeed mature and can come to a resolution on our own."

I smiled at Tyeesha. We officially had a new mediator.

"I'll go first," I said, stepping in when Jasmine still didn't say anything.

"Camille," I said, turning to face her, "no one is ganging up on you. We are so happy for your success. We just want you to remember who was there for you before you made it big."

"Yeah," Jasmine said, finally speaking up. "Who was there when your mom had a heart attack? Who was there when you were crying your eyes out behind Keith, Walter and every other boy you claimed to love?"

"And you've been there for us," Angel added. "Angelica loves you. We just don't want you to lose sight of our friendship."

Camille started tearing up. "You guys," she sniffed, "I will never forget that you're my true friends. Why can't you understand that?"

"Because actions speak louder than words," Jasmine said, a lot more gently than I'd ever expected.

Once Camille stopped being so defensive, we were actually able to have a productive conversation. I was happy to see we'd stopped fighting and were just talking right now. After fifteen minutes, Camille finally said, "Just so you guys know, I'll do better."

Just then Miss Rachel poked her head back in the door. "Are you girls good?"

I waited on someone else to answer, since I was always positive. Tyeesha was the first one. "I'm good!" she exclaimed.

Rachel smiled. "We know you're good. What about the rest of you?"

Still no one spoke. "I'm good," I finally said.

"Me, too," Angel added.

Jasmine shrugged like she didn't really care. I knew that was just her putting her wall up. Jasmine didn't like people treating her wrong, so she was going to carry an attitude a little longer than everyone else.

"I'm good," Camille said, finally breaking out into a wide smile. "And I promise I won't get the big head."

"Again?" Jasmine asked.

"Again," Camille answered. I relaxed as everyone broke out in a smile . . . including Jasmine.

14

Alexis

"So what do you think, Alexis?"

"Huh?" I said, snapping out of my thoughts. Camille had been going on and on for what seemed like an hour now. We were sitting at our regular table in the cafeteria. Camille had started talking right after the bell had rung, and she hadn't shut up since.

I glanced down at my watch. It actually had been only twenty minutes. But my mind definitely wasn't on her drama right now. Granted, I understood that she was going through some things, but so was I. My dad hadn't come home last night, which was pretty major. When I'd asked my mom if he was out of town—the only time he spent the night away from home—she'd simply run into her room crying.

My home life was so miserable. And Camille was going on and on about Xavier.

" . . . I mean, I know why he was mad about the kiss, so I'll give him that, but he didn't have to go talking like I could never measure up to Beyoncé."

"Yeah," I mumbled halfheartedly.

"What is wrong with you?" Camille finally asked.

"I'm sorry, I'm just kinda out of it," I replied. I looked around the cafeteria. "Where's Jasmine and Angel?"

"Jasmine had study hall. Angel had to leave early because Angelica is sick," she said.

"Oh," I sighed heavily. "Where's Tyeesha?"

Camille shrugged and gave me a look like she couldn't care less.

"Camille, you really should give Tyeesha a chance. She's cool."

"She's all right, especially since I know she wasn't trying to talk to Xavier. I'm just not as tight with her as you guys are."

"Maybe we're tight with her because we're giving her a chance." I wanted to remind Camille that she also didn't know Tyeesha because she was never around, but I didn't feel like going there. "Speak of the devil," I said as Tyeesha walked toward us, carrying her lunch tray.

"Hey, hey, hey," she sang. "What's up?" For all the drama she went through at home, she sure had a good attitude. I made a mental note to ask her about it later.

"Hey, girl. Where were you?" I asked.

"I had to take care of some transfer paperwork in the office. They were trying not to count some of my credits, and I wouldn't have been able to graduate. I'm definitely not having that."

"Oh, yeah, I can't imagine that," I said.

"Who you tellin'?" Tyeesha said, taking a seat next to Camille. "So what are y'all talking about?"

"What else?" I rolled my eyes. "Camille and her life."

"Cool. How's it going?" she asked Camille.

That made Camille perk up. "It's going fine. We wrapped up shooting. Now we—"

Tyeesha cut her off as she gazed across the table at me. "Alexis, what's wrong?"

"I just have a lot of stuff on my mind."

"Like what?" Tyeesha asked.

Before I could answer, Camille squealed. "Got a text," she said, pointing toward her cell. "I'll be right back." She jumped up and headed out the door.

Tyeesha immediately turned her attention back to me. "Alexis, I see it all over your face. I mean, I know I don't know you all that well, but I can definitely tell something is wrong."

I took a deep breath, not sure of how much she'd be willing to share. Finally, I said, "You know, you seem like such a happy-go-lucky person."

"I am," she said. "But we're talking about you."

I played with the nasty chicken fingers on my tray. "I was saying that because you mentioned your parents were getting a divorce, and you just seem to, I don't know, take it so well."

Tyeesha didn't agree with that. "I'm okay with it now. I mean, I wasn't at first. That's why I got into all the trouble. I started hanging out with a group of kids my mom hated.

I guess it was my way of acting out. At least that's what the therapist said."

My eyes grew wide. "Wow, you had to go to therapy?"

"Yeah." She nodded. "That shows you that I didn't deal with it well. But I'm okay now. Part of the cure for me was understanding that it's not my fault."

"Why would you blame yourself?"

Tyeesha shrugged. "I don't know. We weren't rich, but we weren't poor either, so there were no fights over money. And it's not like my dad was cheating, at least to my knowledge anyway. They just stopped getting along."

"Wow, that's exactly what's happening to my parents."

"I know, it's a bummer, isn't it?"

"That's why I'm never getting married." I stabbed my chicken fingers with my fork. " 'Cuz that whole 'till death do us part' stuff is a bunch of crap."

"You know, I used to think that, too, but the therapist got me to see things differently."

I shook my head. "That's what I'm seeing, anyway."

"I don't know. I guess I just got okay with it because I know my parents both love me. I really do think they tried their best to make it work, and now, honestly, everybody's happier. It took a minute, but my mother smiles more. My father is happier and—I never, ever thought I'd say this— I'm happier, too. All that fighting and arguing is stressful. Granted, we're staying with my grandmother and her house smells like mothballs, but it's nothing a little Febreze can't cure." She bit into her pizza. "Just hope they can end amicably—I think that's the word the therapist used. Maybe your family should consider therapy."

"Oh, no," I said, thinking how horrified my father would be at the thought of talking to a complete stranger about his problems—if he would even admit that he had a problem. No, I had to come up with another solution. I didn't know what it was, but I had to think of something to keep my parents together.

15

Camille

$\mathcal{I}$ was so excited. It seemed like the whole school was here. We were at Dave & Buster's restaurant for the video-viewing party. Sisco hadn't come because he'd had to fly out for an event in Baltimore tomorrow, but almost everyone else from the set and cast was here. Best of all, they'd pumped it up so that I was actually the star.

Taraji was onstage, singing my praises like she was my best friend. If I didn't know any better, I'd think she really liked me, the way she was up there all grinning and stuff.

"So, ladies and gents, I hope you enjoy 'Just One More Chance' and the star in the making, your very own Camille Simone," Taraji announced. The crowd clapped and I smiled, wondering when she'd changed my name to only my first and middle. But truth be told, I kinda liked it.

I was glad my mom had broken down and let me splurge for the Rocawear outfit I was rocking. I looked too cute in the Karma Camelion off-the-shoulder top and matching In Living Color pants.

I wished Xavier had been here. Even though we hadn't gotten back together, he had spoken to me the other day. Tonight was special and it would have been nice if he'd been here. I totally understood about him not wanting to see me kissing on another boy, even if it had been just an act. But my girls were here, so it was all good. My mom was at work, so she couldn't come, but that probably was for the best as well.

The lights dimmed and the video started playing. There was a lot of oohing and ahhing and clapping. I got a little nervous as the video neared the end. Yeah, Xavier wasn't here, but his boys were, and I had no doubt they'd be giving him a play-by-play account of what happened. And I'm sure they'd give him a hard time about the kiss as well.

I tensed up when it got to the part where Sisco leaned in to kiss me. The girls in the room went wild. I could see Dee and her crew looking at me with pure jealousy. They weren't hating too much, seeing as how they were here. I knew Dee was hoping I sucked, so it would give her something to talk about. I heard she'd been talking about how she should've been the one in the video with Sisco.

Alexis, Jasmine, Angel and even Tyeesha giggled excitedly. I couldn't help but smile—until I looked at the screen and saw Sisco lifting my leg and feeling on my behind. The part that he'd told me would be cut out hadn't been cut at all!

Both the director and Taraji were beaming because the crowd was going crazy. Although Alexis, Jasmine, Tyeesha and Angel were still excited, they were looking at me in shock.

"Dang, you a video vixen for real," Jasmine leaned over and whispered.

I wanted to say something, but I heard a voice behind me hiss, "Camille Simone Harris, have you lost your mind?"

I looked up to see my mom with her eyes wide in horror, her hand clutched to her chest.

"Mama! What are you doing here?" I asked.

She looked around nervously like she was ashamed to be seen with me. "I came to surprise you and share in your special moment." She looked up at the screen as the credits rolled across. "I had no idea I'd be the one surprised."

I was so hoping my mom didn't make a scene. People had already started gathering around me. Even though she was all religious, she kept a level head—most of the time, anyway. Something like this, though, would definitely push her over the edge.

I lowered my voice. "Mom, that was supposed to be cut out."

She glared at me, and I could see the anger and disappointment in her eyes. "If I had known they were going to turn you into some little hoochie, I would've never agreed to this." She eyed the people excitedly waiting to talk to me. "But we'll talk about it when you get home."

She spun around and walked off.

I didn't even have time to be relieved before I heard a loud crash.

"Boy, you know better than running around this place like you ain't got no home training!"

Jasmine groaned, and I immediately recognized her mother's voice.

"Is that your mom?" Alexis asked, peering toward the commotion.

"Yes," Jasmine moaned. The expression on her face said she was about to die of embarrassment. Jasmine's little brother Jalen was getting loudly chastised by his mother. They had been running by the buffet table and had knocked over the trays on the end. A couple of waiters were now hurriedly trying to clean up the mess.

"Man, why did they have to come?" Jasmine groaned. "It's bad enough my mom is working as a waitress here."

When we'd arrived at Dave & Buster's—with Jasmine's two little brothers in tow—Jasmine had nearly had a heart attack when she'd realized the restaurant was the same place her mom worked her second job.

"Where's your grandmother?" Angel asked.

"She had to visit a sick friend at the hospital tonight. So if my brothers didn't come, I couldn't come. Maybe I should've just stayed at home."

If I hadn't been so worried about the video, I would've been just as upset as Jasmine. It was bad enough we'd had to bring her brothers along, but now people were looking at her whole family with disgust, especially when her mother started yelling, "Jasmine, get over here and mind these boys! You're supposed to be watching them!"

"Oh, my God, I'm going to die for real," Jasmine said, trying to hide her face, which wasn't easy, since she was so tall. Jasmine didn't usually get too bothered about what people thought about her, but anyone in their right mind would be embarrassed at the scene that was unfolding here.

"Jasmine!" Ms. Jones called when Jasmine didn't move fast enough. Several people started snickering as Jasmine scurried toward her mother.

"Just ridiculous," Taraji hissed. I didn't even realize she had walked over to me. Before I could come to Jasmine's defense, she broke out in a big fake smile and pointed at the two people next to her.

"Camille, sweetie, I need you. These reporters want to talk to you. I told you you were gonna be a star!" she exclaimed. "This is Erin from the *Defender* and Isiah from one of Houston's most popular blog websites and the *Insite Entertainment* magazine."

All my excitement had waned with all the drama that was unfolding around me, but I tried my best to fake the funk as I talked with the reporters. My friends backed away to give me the limelight.

They asked me a bunch of questions, which were all easy stuff like "how did I feel about this opportunity?" But the last question threw me for a loop.

"So, tell us," Erin said, a mischievous grin across her face, "what's really going on with you and Sisco?"

"Huh?" I said, looking at Taraji. She had a big, goofy grin on her face.

"Come on, give me an exclusive for the magazine," Isiah urged.

"There's nothing to give," I said in confusion. "I'm just in his video."

Erin turned up her lips. "Umm-hmmm. The way you two

were heating up the screen, I know there's something going on. How does it feel to be Sisco's new girl?"

"But I'm n—"

"Okay, that's enough," Taraji said, stepping in and cutting me off. "We have to go. She has to talk with some more people. Thank you guys so much." She eased me away.

Part of me wanted to protest some more, but the other was grateful that Taraji had saved me. I was beginning to feel more and more like maybe I wasn't cut out for this lifestyle at all. I looked around for my girls, but they were gone. I couldn't even go look for them, because I was surrounded by all my new fans. I knew I was definitely going to hear about this later.

16

Camille

After the crowd died down, I tried to talk to the director about why he kept the scene with Sisco feeling on me. He'd looked at me like he'd no idea what I'd been talking about. I knew right then that Sisco hadn't said a word to him.

"Camille, you know I am not happy," my mother said. I was so lost in thought that I hadn't even heard her come into my bedroom. She was on the phone when I'd gotten home. I was about to knock on her door, but then I'd heard her say into the phone, "I know, I am just so ashamed. Did Christi tell you everything?"

I had eased away from her door. She'd been talking to her friend Mrs. Judy from church. Of course, Judy's bigmouthed, messy daughter Christi had run home and told her mom everything.

My mother was dressed in a yellow flowered housecoat. Half her hair was adorned with pink hair rollers, like she'd started rolling her hair and gotten sidetracked by the phone conversation. I was hoping she would just finish rolling her hair and go on to bed. Of course, I had no such luck.

"Mom, it's no big deal," I said.

She stood with her hands planted firmly on her hips. "If you were someone else's child, maybe it wouldn't be. Do you know I barely got in the door before Judy was calling to talk about that horrible video my child was in? I know she's called half the folks in the church by now."

"That's all you care about, how you look to your church members," I mumbled as I stepped into my lounging pajamas.

"Okay, you're about to get smacked in the mouth," my mother said. Despite always threatening to, she had never actually hit me in the mouth. Still, I had no doubt that she would.

"I'm sorry," I muttered, looking up at her. "It's just that this was supposed to be the best day of my life. Now you're mad, Xavier is mad. It's just a disaster." I plopped down on my bed.

My mother sat down on the edge of my mattress. She hesitated a few moments before saying, "Camille, why do you think I'm upset about that video?" Her voice was remarkably calm.

I shrugged. "Because I'm kissing a boy?"

She nodded sadly. "Yes, but most of all because you're better than that. It's bad enough that they have you looking like a hooker in those clothes, but then you allow that boy to feel all over you in a video that's going to play all over the country. That is just disrespectful."

"Mom, I was acting," I protested. She was making it seem like I was just out on the street letting some guy do me any old kind of way.

"No, you were allowing someone to disrespect you. It's about having standards that say, 'I'm not going to let you degrade me or my body'—even in the name of music." She sighed like she couldn't understand why I wasn't getting it. "You know, think about the young girls you mentor at that elementary school—what is it?"

"Kennedy," I said, wondering where this life lesson was going.

"What type of message do you think those young girls will walk away with if they see you up on that screen like that?"

I thought about it. They'd understand that it was just a video. I mean, I didn't really like it but I figured Sisco's fans would understand.

"But videos are images. And images shape perceptions—how people see you."

My mom must've known I still wasn't getting it, because she continued, "Why do you think I hate most rap music?"

I frowned. "All parents hate rap music."

She exhaled in frustration. "No. I hate music that disrespects and degrades our women. That's what that video did. I'm working hard to raise you into a smart young woman who respects herself enough to demand respect from others. And if you don't respect yourself, how can you expect anyone else to do it?"

"Sisco respects me," I said. This conversation was really getting on my nerves. "Shoot, I didn't even like him feeling me up, but what was I supposed to do?"

"You should have voiced your disapproval. Your silence told him it was okay."

"I asked him to have that part taken out," I protested. "It's not my fault he didn't. Besides, what's the big deal anyway? Most people just listen to the beat."

My mother stood up, tired of arguing with me. "That's the problem. You young girls want to just blame it on the music and say, 'Oh, no one is listening to the words' while the rapper calls you all kinds of disrespectful names. Then you wonder why you can't get young men to show you respect."

She shook her head in pity, like she felt sorry for my generation.

"Just think about what I'm saying," my mother said as she headed toward my door. She stopped right before she stepped into the hallway. "And oh, yeah, I will be calling that video director tomorrow. You might not have enough respect for yourself to see something is wrong with that video, but I do."

I fell back on my bed. Being in this video was supposed to have been the best thing that had ever happened to me. So why was it turning into such a nightmare?

17

Camille

I got the text, and all it said was *Meet me by the gym lockers as soon as you get here!! Jasmine.*

Since Jasmine didn't have a cell phone, she must have borrowed someone else's to send me the text. That meant I couldn't text her back to find out what was up. But judging by the exclamation points at the end, it was major.

I was speed-walking toward the gym. When I rounded the corner and saw Jasmine, Tyeesha, Angel and Alexis huddled together, I knew something was going on.

"What's up?" I asked as I approached them.

They slowly broke up their circle. "Have you seen the paper?" Angel asked.

"What paper? The school newspaper? It doesn't come out

until Friday." I wondered why they were asking me that. Everyone knew when our school paper came out.

"No, the *Insite,* that tabloid newspaper," Alexis said.

"No, I haven't seen it." I broke out in a huge smile when I noticed the paper in Jasmine's hand. "Oh wow, do they have something in there about me? Let me see it."

"Oh, it has something in here about you, all right," Jasmine said, handing the paper to me.

As I took it, the smile immediately left my face. On the front page was a photo of me and Sisco, kissing, his hand positioned on my behind. It was a still photo taken from the video shoot. The caption read, "Sisco's New Freak of the Week?" I read the article out loud. " 'Sources say mega rapper Sisco has a new love in his life, the new girl from his video, Camille Simone, and this time she's more than just his freak . . . ' What?" I said, looking up dumbfounded. "What is this?"

Everybody raised their eyebrows, but nobody said anything.

"Where'd you get this from?" I asked.

"Dee had it this morning," Angel said. "She had a bunch of copies and she was passing them out to people."

I groaned in horror. Of course Dee would do that. "Who are the sources?" I asked, quickly scanning the article again. "It says I dumped Xavier after spending some private time in Sisco's dressing room." I looked up in shock. "Oh, my God! That didn't happen! Why would they print this?"

"I don't know, but if Dee had it this morning, you can rest assured that it was just a matter of time before Xavier gets it," Jasmine said.

My heart dropped. Xavier. Now I would never get back right with him.

"Why would they do this?" I cried.

"I don't know," Alexis said, "but that looks pretty bad, Camille. Even worse than it did on the screen."

"Who are you telling?" I said, feeling the tears welling up in my eyes. I looked so . . . cheap, with his hand all over my behind. "There's nothing going on between us," I mumbled, "and this picture is just so degrading."

"Yeah, it makes you look like a hoochie," Jasmine said.

Alexis elbowed her sharply. "What?" Jasmine said. "It does." A sympathetic look crossed her face. "I'm sorry, I mean, we know you're not a hoochie. But that picture is jacked up."

I was just about to say something when I noticed Xavier and his boys walking toward us.

"Oh, snap," I said, stuffing the newspaper in my backpack.

Xavier was smiling and laughing with his friends, which must've meant he hadn't seen the paper yet.

"Hey," I said when he approached us.

"Hey," he replied. He was still a little salty, but at least he seemed in an okay mood.

"Wh—what are you guys doing?" I stammered.

"Ummm, about to go to class," his friend Joshua said. "It is the beginning of the school day. What's wrong with you? You look like you've seen a ghost."

"What? Naw," I casually said. "I just—I guess I didn't sleep too well."

Jasmine cleared her throat and nodded down the hall. I turned to see where she was pointing. Dee and her crew were sashaying toward me. And from the looks on their faces, they were coming to start some mess.

"Okay, we'll let you guys go," I said too brightly. "You don't wanna be late."

"Are you sure you're okay?" Xavier asked.

"Yeah, yeah, I'm fine," I said, pushing him down the hall.

"All right," he said. "We're out." They had just walked off when Dee called out to him.

"Xavier!" she said, purring his name.

He stopped and turned around to face her. "What's up, Dee?"

"Nothing much," she said, stopping in front of him. Of course, she didn't bother to speak to me—or anyone else, for that matter.

"How are you?" She sounded so fake.

"I'm straight," Xavier said, confused. "Why?"

She shrugged. "I was just wondering how you were holding up."

He looked back at his boys. "What do you mean?"

"I just thought you'd be a little upset," she said. She was really enjoying herself.

"Why would I be upset?" He glanced over at me. "Oh, you mean about the video. I'm straight."

"Come on, Xavier, let's go," I said, trying to grab his arm to pull him away. I wanted to leave before things got too bad. "I need to talk to you."

Dee snatched the paper from her friend and thrust it at Xavier. "Upset about this," she said, flashing the front page of the paper. I wanted to just knock her in her jaw, but I was frozen in place. It had to happen sometime.

"Dang!" Joshua yelled, peering at the paper over Xavier's shoulder.

"I know, huh?" Dee said, all innocently. "Most guys wouldn't be all nice if their girlfriend left them for a rapper."

"Dee, why don't you go on somewhere?" Jasmine finally said, coming to my defense.

"Okay." She pushed the paper toward Xavier. "You keep that as a little token. And my number is written at the top in case you need to call me"—she turned her nose up at me—"and vent. I'll be your shoulder to cry on." I know she didn't even want Xavier. She was just trying to get under my skin.

Dee patted his cheek, then walked off.

Xavier continued staring at the paper, dumbfounded.

"Xavier, I—"

"Did you know about this?" he asked.

"No." I don't know why the lie was the first thing out of my mouth, but it was.

Just then Joshua reached down in my backpack and snatched out the newspaper I'd stuffed in there. "So then why do you have your own copy?"

I cut my eyes at him.

"So now you his freak?" Xavier said, not taking his eyes off the paper. "And you dumped me for him? When were you going to tell me this?"

"No, it's not like that at all," I protested.

Xavier read some more of the article, then threw the paper at me and stormed off.

"Xavier, wait." Frantic, I followed him.

He stopped, spun around and glared at me. "Camille, if you know what's best for you, you will get away from me."

That look in his eyes was one I'd never seen before. This

could really be the end for us. I hurried down the hall, wanting to speak in private with him.

I finally got him to stop on the side of the gym.

"This is all just publicity stuff, you know, to pump up the album." I knew I was just rehashing what Taraji had said, even though I didn't believe it myself. But I was desperate to say anything to get through to Xavier.

"Camille, I don't care what it is. This looks really trashy!"

I was starting to get sick of defending myself. I'd told him how I felt.

"Why do you have a problem with what I'm trying to do?"

He gritted his teeth in frustration. "You just don't get it, do you?"

I folded my arms across my chest. Now he was working my nerve, too. "Maybe you just can't handle my fame."

He stared at me, then busted out laughing. "Your *fame*? Are you serious?"

When I didn't smile, he continued, "You know what, you and your *fame,* and your new boyfriend . . ." He held his hands up to calm himself down. "All y'all can have each other 'cuz I'm out."

"What is that supposed to mean?"

"It means just what I said. I'm done. And this time I mean it." He started walking off.

"I can't believe you're acting like this," I said, following him. "You're the one who pushed me to be in the talent show in the first place."

He stopped and turned around. "If I had known winning would turn you into this diva, I wouldn't have wasted my breath."

"Oh, so now I'm a diva?"

He paused. "Naw, I take that back. You're a *wannabe* diva. Holla at me when the old Camille comes back." He looked me up and down with disgust. "That's if she doesn't get lost in the *fame.*"

With that, he stomped off, and this time I didn't try and stop him.

18

Alexis

I felt like I was in the middle of World War Three. If I wasn't surrounded by fighting and bickering at home, I had to deal with it at school. Now it had crossed over into the only place where I had any peace—my Good Girlz meetings.

Jasmine and Camille were going at it like crazy. Tyeesha had given up trying to referee, and both she and Angel were just staring as Jasmine and Camille went back and forth arguing.

"I don't blame him for dumping you!" Jasmine yelled. "We don't even know who you are anymore!" It had only been three weeks since Camille had won the talent show, and she'd become somebody we didn't even half recognize. After the video release party everybody had been giving her props. She'd been on two TV stations, and the newspaper had done a feature on her. It was like all of the attention had gone to her head. Even that trashy tabloid story hadn't changed things.

"I can't believe you said that!" Camille responded. "Number one, Xavier didn't dump me. I dumped him. And number two, I'm the same person I was before! You all are the ones that are changing!"

I tried my best to tune them out, but after a few more minutes I had had enough. "Shut up!" I screamed at the top of my lungs. "Would you both just shut up? I'm so sick of this!"

My outburst caught everyone by surprise. They all fell instantly silent, staring at me.

"What in the world is going on in here? Why are you all screaming like you've lost your minds?" Miss Rachel walked in the room, clearly irritated. She looked like she was about to really go off when she took a good look at me. "Alexis, why are you crying?"

I didn't even realize I was crying. I just felt exhausted, because it seemed everybody I loved was at each other's throats.

"I don't know," I said, feeling drained. "I'm just tired. Everybody is so caught up in this trivial stuff. You know, other people do have things going on in their lives besides videos and stupid arguments," I spat at my friends. "You guys make me sick!" I stood up and ran out of the room.

Miss Rachel followed me into the hallway. I'm sure everyone was freaking out, because I never had dramatic outbursts. Miss Rachel caught up with me and grabbed my arm. "Alexis, let's go in my office and talk."

"I don't want to talk." I was fed up and I wanted everybody to leave me alone. I still hadn't come up with a plan to keep my parents together, and judging from the fact that my dad hadn't come home again last night, my time was running out. That was the only thing I was concerned about.

"Can you do it for me?" Miss Rachel asked softly.

Since she put it like that, I didn't feel like I had much choice. Maybe talking to an adult would do me good. Maybe she could help me come up with a plan. As I followed Miss Rachel into her office, her husband, Reverend Adams, was just walking out.

"Hi, sweetheart. I put those papers on your desk." He leaned over and kissed her on the cheek.

She nodded, then he turned to me. "Hello, Alexis, how are you?"

"Fine," I mumbled.

They must have done some husband and wife mental stuff, because he said, "I'll keep you in my prayers," then gently squeezed my hand before walking off.

Miss Rachel took a seat in the chair in front of her desk, then motioned for me to sit down in the one next to her. I did, and she gently took my hand. "You know, Alexis, your journey with the Good Girlz hasn't been easy," she began. "For all of you. But I'd like to think we've learned some valuable lessons along the way."

"I have," I admitted.

"Well, that learning process is never over. To this day, I'm still learning."

"Learning what?" I asked, surprised by this confession.

"To control my emotions, not let them rule my actions." An odd look passed over her face. I couldn't quite make it out, and she quickly shook it off and kept talking. "The bottom line remains, I'm a work in progress. So having said that, I think it's really okay for you to blow off a little steam every now and then. What concerns me is that you are always so good-natured. I'd really like to know what's bothering you to the point of losing it."

I blew out a long breath as I thought about what Tyeesha had said. "Miss Rachel, can I ask you a question?"

"Of course."

"I remember one Sunday I was watching church on TV and hearing the pastor say that God hates divorce. Does that mean if you get a divorce, God can't forgive you?" I know I was shifting nervously, but I was uncomfortable talking about this.

Miss Rachel smiled. "Well, first of all, we need to talk about you *watching* church and not going to church." She winked and continued. "But you heard right, God hates divorce. He loves divorced people, though. His love doesn't stop because you do something He doesn't like."

That was encouraging. "I don't mean to get in your business, but have you ever thought about divorcing Reverend Adams?" I asked. I didn't want to cross into her personal life, but I just needed to feel like I wasn't in this alone.

Miss Rachel was straight with me, like always. "It's no secret to anyone at Zion Hill that I've not only thought about it but even took steps in that direction."

"Did you ever think about what it would do to your kids?"

"Of course I did. My children love Lester, and they would've been heartbroken if I had divorced him. But I wouldn't have made that decision unless I was sure that in the long run it was better for everyone." That didn't sit well with me, and she noticed my sour face. "But I don't want to talk about me. I want to talk about you."

"My parents may be getting a divorce," I blurted out. "And I've got to come up with a way to stop them."

Miss Rachel nodded, finally understanding. "Sweetie, you have to trust that everything your parents do will be done in love."

I just didn't get that. If they loved me, they'd stay together. It was that simple. "Do you think I could've done something differently?" I asked. "Maybe if I had cooperated more, if I didn't get in any trouble, if I had better grades . . ." My voice trailed off.

"Alexis, you have a four-point-zero. How much better can your grades get?" Miss Rachel replied, taking my hand. "And remember, you came to the Good Girlz because you wanted to, not because you had to. You are a wonderful child that any parent would love to have. I don't know your parents' personal business, but I doubt very seriously that you contributed in any shape, form or fashion to their divorce."

I sighed. I heard what she was saying, but I didn't know if I believed it. One thing I did know—this divorce couldn't happen. And I wouldn't rest until I made sure that it didn't.

19

Camille

I was so tired of fighting with my friends, but I didn't know what to do. Thoughts of my argument with Jasmine and my breakup with Xavier were eating me alive. But I'd promised Maya that I'd come with her and two other dancers, named Shandy and Keke, to the *America's Next Top Model* auditions at the Galleria Mall. Both Maya and Shandy thought they were shoo-ins for the show.

"Girl, why are you sitting up in here looking like you lost your best friend?" Maya asked.

"What's wrong?" Shandy asked as she walked up behind Maya.

"I'm all right," I said. I had only talked to Maya that one time I'd been fighting with Xavier, but I remembered how she had made me feel better. Since I needed to talk to someone about everything I was going through, I thought I might as well talk to someone who understood this business.

"Do you mind if I ask you guys something? How do you all do it, you know, do the video thing and manage your friends and your boyfriend and stuff?"

Shandy giggled. "These are my friends," she said, motioning to Maya and Keke.

"Yeah," Maya added. "When you try to hang with people who ain't in the business, it's nothing but drama. I told you that."

"Not to mention the fact that you have to worry about people being with you just because you're famous," Keke added.

I thought back to my conversation with Xavier the other day. "I'm hardly famous," I said. The more I thought about it, the more I realized the whole "fame" comment might have been a bit much.

"Not yet," Shandy said. "But trust me, you're on your way. Girl, you can sing."

"And say what you want," Maya added, "if you're in a Sisco video, you're famous. You might not be superstar status, but you've got a lot more going for you than these other busters."

Shandy fluffed out her honey brown curly weave. "You just have to be careful," she said. "Your friends are probably just jockin' you anyway, tryin' to see what they can get."

"Oh, no, my friends aren't like that," I countered.

All three of the girls exchanged knowing looks. "That's what we all used to think," Shandy said.

"Was that one of your friends at the release party?" Keke asked. "The one whose brothers knocked over the buffet table and whose mama was acting all ghetto?"

I nodded. "That's my best friend, Jasmine. But we've . . . things . . . let's just say they aren't too good right now."

They all groaned and rolled their eyes. "Gimme a break," Shandy moaned.

"Truth be told, you need to be finding a new set of friends anyway," Maya added.

"What?" I said. Yeah, I was mad at my girls, but I wasn't trying to get rid of them.

"Let me break it down to you," Maya said, like she was really trying to school me. "Those girls are no longer in your league. You got that ol' homely-looking one with the long black hair."

"Angel?" I asked.

"Whatever her name is." Maya shrugged like she couldn't care less.

"Didn't I hear her say she had a kid? A two-year-old? Isn't she like fifteen?" Shandy added.

I was quick to defend her. "No, she's sixteen, almost seventeen."

"So that means she had a kid at what, fourteen, fifteen? Please." Shandy threw up her hands. "You have an image to think about now."

"And don't even get me started on that other one, Jasmine. Talk about ghetto. As if you need that." Maya dramatically rolled her eyes.

I was dumbfounded. I couldn't believe they were talking about my friends like that. They must've realized how I was feeling, because Shandy gently touched my arm and said, "Look, we're just keepin' it real with you. In this business, you are the company you keep."

"That's right," Maya echoed, "and if you want to get invited to all the hottest parties, get hired for more videos and even get your own shot at the big time, it's all about being with the right people in the right place at the right time. Houston is about to become the new Hollywood. All the rappers and singers are coming here to shoot their videos, and if you want in, you gotta be in it to win it."

I couldn't believe what they were saying. If I wanted to make it in this business, I had to abandon my friends? That was crazy.

"And don't even get me started on that boyfriend of yours," Maya continued.

"Ex," I said sadly.

"Y'all broke up?" Shandy asked.

I nodded.

"Good, you need to keep it that way," Maya replied. "Because another thing you won't have a shortage of is cute boys tryin' to holla at you."

I didn't know what to say. I knew this business was brutal, but now I was learning that if I wanted to truly be a star, it was going to come at a serious cost—my friendship with the Good Girlz. Was that really the price of fame? And was it a price I was willing to pay?

20

Alexis

"*Ugggh!*" I released a loud, frustrated groan. I already had my music as high up as it would go. The sounds of Lil' Wayne bounced off the walls of my oversized pink bedroom.

I knew this fight was serious. If Lil' Wayne wasn't enough to get my mom to come barreling into my room, ordering me to "turn that crap off," something had to be really wrong.

But then again, who was I kidding? I knew something was wrong. It had been wrong for a while. All my parents ever did these days was argue. And that whole divorce thing my mom had been talking about was looking more and more like a reality.

I knocked my history book off my bed, grabbed the pillow and put it over my head. I had a geography test tomorrow, and even if I hadn't had the music blaring, I wouldn't have been able to study anyway. My parents had been going at it for over an hour now. This was one of their worst fights ever. I so wished Sonja was here.

I picked up my phone to call Camille. She was the one person who could always make me feel better when my parents fought. I knew she'd been super busy, but I really needed her right now.

"Hello," she said, answering on the first ring.

Before I could get a sound out, I started crying.

"Alexis?"

"Camille, I need to talk to you," I said through my tears. "It's my parents. All the fighting, it's just getting to be too much, and I think it's just a matter of time before—"

"Alexis?" she repeated. "Is that you? I can't hear you. What's all that noise?"

I hadn't even paid attention to the fact that my iPod was still blasting Lil' Wayne.

"Oh, hold on a minute," I began, but she cut me off again.

"If you can hear me, I'll call you back. I'm babysitting and these kids are out of control."

"Wait, Camille, I really—" She hung up the phone before I could finish my sentence.

I was so upset that I just pushed the End button, then dialed Jasmine's number.

"Hello," Jasmine said.

"Hey, Jasmine," I said.

"Hel-lo!" Jasmine repeated. "Alexis, is that you?" she yelled. "Why is it so loud? Are you at the club or something?"

I groaned, reached over, grabbed the remote and hit the mute button on my iPod system.

"What's up, girl? And why you got the music blasting like that? Was that Lil' Wayne?"

"Yeah, it's his new album. The uncut version."

"Ooooh, your parents must definitely not be at home."

"Yeah, they are." They were definitely making that clear. "But it's not like it matters. It's not like my parents will stop fighting long enough to even notice."

Jasmine's tone softened. "Dang, they're fighting again?"

"Yes," I said, fighting back tears. "And I don't understand. How do you go from being so in love to hating each other?"

"I'm sure they don't hate each other."

I listened to yet another door slam. "That's sure not love." I couldn't make out what my mom was saying, but she was being her usual dramatic self and screaming at the top of her lungs.

I imagined my father. He was usually calm and cool, but my mom must've been pushing his buttons, because he was yelling as well.

"I just wish . . ." I couldn't even finish my sentence before I was crying again.

"Awww, Alexis, don't cry," Jasmine said. "Hold on, I'm going to call Angel and Camille so we can cheer you up."

"I just called Camille. She's busy."

Jasmine didn't sound surprised by that news. "Well, hang on while I call Angel." I held the phone and tried to stop my tears while she clicked over.

"Hey, Angel," I said, my voice wading in tears, when they both were on the line.

"Hey, Alexis, you okay?" Angel asked.

"No," I whimpered.

"Awww, sweetie, I'm sorry," Angel said. "You want us to come over? My mom's here, so she can watch Angelica. And we can call Camille and Tyeesha to meet us there. We can just have one big slumber party."

"Alexis already talked to Camille. She's busy," Jasmine said, not trying to hide her sarcasm.

"Oh, that's right," Angel replied. "My sister said she saw her at the Galleria Mall for the *America's Next Top Model* auditions."

"What?" Jasmine exclaimed. "When?"

"Probably about fifteen minutes ago," Angel replied. "That's how long Rosario has been home. She said she saw her coming in the mall with some older girls as she was leaving. She said one of them had a number on her chest for the auditions. Why?"

A few beats of silence passed before Jasmine said, "Because Camille told Alexis she was babysitting."

"For real?" Angel replied.

"Yeah, but maybe I misunderstood," I said, even though I knew I had heard her loud and clear.

"Yeah, right," Jasmine said. "Well, we'll just see about that. Hold on." We all waited while Jasmine called Camille. Jasmine clicked back over once she had Camille on the line. "What's up, Jaz?" Camille said.

"Hey, where are you?" Jasmine asked.

"Why?"

"Because Alexis and Angel are on the phone. Alexis is going through it, and we need to go over there."

Camille hesitated, then said, "Dang, um, I . . . I can't."

"And why not?" Jasmine asked.

"I . . . I'm babysitting my neighbor's kids."

We all were silent for a moment. Jasmine finally said, "You're babysitting?"

"Yeah, and girl, these kids are bad. I finally got them to sleep."

"So, they're 'sleep now?" Jasmine slowly asked.

"Yeah. I've been here all day, and their mom won't be back until tonight."

"Is that right?" Jasmine asked. I knew she was thinking the same thing I was. Why was Camille telling us a bold-faced lie?

"Yeah," Camille replied. "So, let me get off this phone and go check on them."

"Yeah, you do that," Jasmine said.

Camille either didn't notice the sarcasm in Jasmine's voice or didn't care. All I could think about was the fact that she hadn't even bothered to ask me what was wrong.

"I can't believe she just straight-up lied," Angel said once Camille hung up the phone.

"How long ago did your sister say she saw her at the mall?" Jasmine asked.

"Rosario just got home. She said she saw Camille going in the mall with a bunch of girls as she was coming out."

"Maybe she only stayed a minute, then went to go baby-sit," I said, not believing it myself.

"Maybe the kids are sleeping in the furniture section of Macy's," Jasmine said dryly.

I was stunned. Camille had done some dirty things when she'd been trying out for this teen talk show on Channel 2 last year, but she'd apologized like crazy, and she'd changed.

But maybe, just maybe, this newfound stardom had caused her to change right back.

21

Alexis

I really did not have a good feeling about this, but Jasmine was adamant that we all go to the mall. She said she was fed up with Camille and her ways, and we had to call her on it.

"Jasmine, do you really think this is a good idea?" I said as we made our way into the Galleria Mall. Jasmine had been so pumped that she'd asked her older sister to drop her off, and she didn't ask her sister for anything. I'd swung by and picked up Angel, and now we were heading inside.

There had to be a thousand people here. Camille loved *America's Next Top Model*, so it didn't surprise me that she would be here trying out for it. Looking at all of the people, I wondered how Jasmine thought we were ever going to find Camille.

Surprisingly, we'd only been searching the crowd for a minute when Angel said, "There she is."

Jasmine and I both looked to where Angel was pointing. Camille was sitting on the front row next to a girl I recognized from the video. I could not believe my eyes. I had been holding out hope that this was all a big misunderstanding.

"See, I told you," Jasmine said, anger burning in her voice. "If it's one thing I can't stand, it's when somebody tries to play me. And I'm about to go tell Camille about herself."

"No, wait," I said, grabbing Jasmine's arm. "Do you really want to make a scene in front of all these people?"

"I don't care about these people," Jasmine snorted.

"Come on, Jaz, chill," Angel said. "Let's just hang back and wait for them to get up."

I couldn't tell if they were auditioning until I saw another girl walk back over to them and rip a number from her chest. Judging from the furious look on her face, she hadn't been picked. She motioned for Camille and the other two girls to come on, and then she stomped ahead of them.

"Jasmine, I don't know about this. Maybe we should just talk to Camille later," I said.

Jasmine didn't respond. She was already heading over to intercept Camille. She stopped just as Camille was turning the corner.

"Camille!" Jasmine called out.

Camille spun around, as did the other girls. Camille's mouth dropped open when she saw us.

"So, how are the kids?" Jasmine said sarcastically.

"Man, that's foul," Angel said. "Now you're lying to us?"

I was still speechless.

"Hey, uh, uh . . . ," Camille stammered.

"Uh, uh, what?" Jasmine said.

"Camille, is there a problem?" the girl from the video said.

"Naw, Maya, um, these are my fr—the girls I go to school with."

We all looked at her, dumbfounded. Now we'd been downgraded to classmates?

"Yeah, there's a problem," Jasmine said, eyeing Maya up and down. "You're in our conversation."

"Excuse me?" Maya said.

"Yeah, excuse you," Jasmine responded before turning back to Camille. "So, what's up?"

"Yeah, Camille, I thought you said you were babysitting?" Angel added.

Camille looked like she was searching for a lie. But she didn't get a chance to say anything, because the girl who'd ripped off the number stepped in. "She told us all about y'all and I told her you're crampin' her image. So maybe she lied because she was trying to spare your feelings. Maybe she doesn't like hanging around with wannabes," she said, looking me up and down, "teenage baby mamas," she said, looking at Angel, or "hood rats," she said, turning back to Jasmine.

I cringed as I saw Jasmine's nostrils flare. I couldn't care less what she said about me, but she'd crossed the line talking about Jasmine and Angel. Maybe this was the new group of people Camille was hanging out with, but I could not believe that she would stand there and let them go off like that. I couldn't believe she had told them that stuff about us, because there was no other way they could've known. I was tempted to let Jasmine do Jasmine, but since I wasn't in the mood for anyone to get arrested, I put my hand on Jasmine's arm.

"Unh-unh, let me go," she said, snatching her arm away. "This chick got me messed up. I will yank that weave right out of your head."

"And you'll get yours yanked right back," the girl said.

Jasmine swung her ponytail, which had grown tremendously over the last year and now hung down her back. "It's real, which is more than I can say about anything on you."

"Oh, you ain't the only one from the hood," Maya said. "The difference is, we know how to turn it on and off. But it ain't nothing but a thang for us to turn it on." She started removing her earrings.

"Camille, what's going on?" I said, outraged that she would let this happen.

"Guys, please," Camille finally said. "Let me handle this."

"Yeah, handle it, Camille," Maya said. "Because this is exactly what I'm talking about. This is the kind of stuff you don't need. I told you, you really need to leave these busters alone."

"I got your busters," Jasmine said, taking another step forward.

"Camille?" Angel pleaded. By now people were starting to stare. I even caught a few people pointing their camera phones at us like they were waiting for a fight to jump off.

"Guys, I'm sorry I told you I was babysitting. It's just . . . ," Camille began.

"It's just she didn't want to be bothered," one of the girls chimed in.

"Shandy, please!" Camille said. "Can you guys go on? I'll catch up with you in a minute."

Shandy rolled her eyes. "Come on, Maya. Let's go before these girls make me act straight ig'nant up in this mall. I'm already mad about them picking all these ugly girls over me." They walked off, Shandy still griping.

We all stood staring at Camille.

"So, it's like that now, huh?" Jasmine said.

"Camille, why'd you lie?" Angel asked.

"Guys, I'm so sorry," Camille said, ashamed. "It's just that I knew I was coming here with them, and I didn't know what to tell you."

"How 'bout the truth?" Jasmine snapped. "It's not like we would've been surprised, because you don't have time for us anyway."

"See, this is exactly what I'm talking about," Camille huffed. "I knew it would be drama."

"You know what, Camille?" I said, speaking up. "Don't even worry about it. You don't want the drama. Our drama. So you go on and enjoy your life as Sisco's sidekick or whatever it is you have going on. You kick it with your new friends, and you don't have to worry about us anymore."

Camille's face hardened. "Why you gotta be all dramatic?"

"It is what it is," I said, feeling teary-eyed all over again.

"You know," Jasmine said, gritting her teeth, "the fact that you got Alexis upset ought to tell you how jacked up this is."

Jasmine was right. It took a whole lot to push my buttons, and Camille had pushed me right over the edge. I was too through.

Camille's eyes started watering up as well. "I just wish you'd understand."

"Oh, we understand loud and clear," Jasmine said. "Alexis

is going through it. All she wanted was to talk to you. But you gotta try and play her."

"I'm sorry. Alexis, what's wrong?" Camille asked, looking concerned.

Before I could answer, Maya yelled, "Camille, let's go."

"I'm coming!" Camille yelled back. She turned back to me. "Seriously, what's going on? Why are you upset?"

I let out a pained laugh. That new girl's timing couldn't have been more perfect. "You know what, Camille? Don't even worry about it. Your friends are waiting."

Jasmine looked Camille up and down in disgust, turned around and walked off. Even Angel said, "Wow, Camille, that's really messed up."

Me, I had no words left. I just looked her dead in the eye, trying to see who this person was standing before me. I used to think that I wanted to be famous, but if this is what it turned you into, forget it. I couldn't say anything else as I turned to go catch up with my friends—my real friends.

22

Camille

I was getting to the point where I hated coming to school. Sure, people were still jocking me and giving me props about the video, which had begun playing regularly on BET and MTV. But a few others had started calling me derogatory names, thinking it was funny. For the most part, I tried to ignore their heckling.

I'd missed the last two Good Girlz meetings, since that blowup with Jasmine last week. I'd pretty much kept to myself, going to school, then practice with Sisco, because we were supposed to be performing at this hip-hop honors show being filmed in Houston at the end of next month.

"Hi, Camille, you going to the play?" this girl named

Veronica said, snapping me out of my thoughts. Before I could answer, the bell rang to dismiss class.

I nodded. "Yeah, I'm headed there now."

I had almost bailed out of attending because Xavier was in the play, but I'd get extra credit for my creative English class. Since I'd gotten an F for not turning in my last assignment, I made my way to the auditorium.

I felt strange, because I usually sat with Jasmine, Alexis and Angel at school events. But now I was all by myself. After our argument, I'd told them all where they could go, and I'd stormed out. Now I wished I had waited around to find out what was up with Alexis, but I'd been so mad at Jasmine that I had just had to get out of there.

I immediately noticed Jasmine, Alexis, Angel and Tyeesha on the left side of the auditorium, laughing and giggling. The fact that they hadn't bothered to save a seat for me told me I wasn't welcome, so I sat next to Veronica.

Luckily, the play started pretty quickly. It was actually pretty good. It was called *On a Wing and Prayer*. The only downside was the fact that Dee was in it, too. But still, I found myself getting caught up in the drama.

That is, until the final scene. That's when Xavier reached over and kissed Dee. I felt my heart drop into the pit of my stomach.

On the side of the stage, the drama teacher loudly cleared her throat. Xavier laughed and pulled away from Dee. "Sorry, I got carried away." Dee giggled but continued her scene.

I don't know how the play ended—everything from the kiss on was a blur. All I could think of was getting up and running out, but I didn't want anyone to see me.

As soon as the play ended, I made a beeline to the door.

I raced to the parking lot, hoping my mom was waiting outside. This was definitely one of those times I wanted my car, as raggedy as it was. If I'd had it, I would've been long gone.

I couldn't believe how long my mom was taking. I was about to call her when I heard Dee's voice. "Hey, Camille, how'd you like the play?"

I closed my eyes, willing her to go away. I turned around and there she was, standing with her arm around Xavier's waist.

I took a deep breath. I was determined not to let them know they'd gotten to me.

"It was no Tyler Perry production, but it was all right," I said, shrugging halfheartedly.

"What?" she asked. "You mean you didn't like Xavier's spontaneous kiss?"

I cut my eyes at him. I knew he was mad at me, but how could he be that cruel?

"Whatever, Dee," I said, turning back around. I so wished my mom would hurry up.

I noticed Jasmine, Alexis, Angel and Tyeesha heading my way. I knew things were bad, but I was thankful to see them. Anything to get away from Dee and Xavier. I smiled at them and was getting ready to say something when they flashed hateful expressions. Even Angel was looking at me all funky. Then they walked right past me without saying a word.

I heard Dee snickering. "Looks like no one wants you anymore."

"Shut up, Dee," I hissed.

"Or what?" she said, dropping her arm from around

Xavier's waist. Her girls were right behind her. Angel looked back and noticed me and Dee about to get into it. She even hesitated like she wanted to come say something, but in the end, she just kept walking toward Alexis's car.

"Just leave me alone," I finally said. I retreated farther down the sidewalk. I wasn't a fighter, but if she followed me down the sidewalk, it was on.

She wasn't the one, though, who ended up following me.

"Yo, Camille, wait up."

I looked back to see Xavier heading my way. Dee was standing there, mad, her arms folded across her chest.

"What, Xavier?" I said. "I'm sure your new girlfriend doesn't appreciate you leaving her to come talk to me."

"Look," he said, "I know me kissing Dee was messed up. But I just wanted you to see how it felt."

It hurt. Like crazy. But I wasn't about to tell him that.

"I mean, did it make it all right because I was acting?" he continued.

It didn't. But I didn't say a word.

"Well, that's how I felt when you did the video."

"So, this was payback?" I shook my head, not giving in. "You do what you want. You made it clear we were through."

"We are," he said matter-of-factly, "but I don't want you to think I'm some kind of dog. You played me."

"I didn't play you, Xavier," I said, softening.

"Whatever you want to call it. The bottom line is, you chose this new world over me. And from what I hear, you chose it over your friends as well."

I rolled my eyes. "Whatever."

He gave me a disbelieving look. He knew me too well. "Camille, you had some good people in your life. You need to think about that and ask yourself if fame is worth the price you're paying."

He shook his head, pitying me, before making his way back over to Dee. I fought back tears as Angel, Alexis, Jasmine and Tyeesha passed by in Alexis's car. They were laughing about something. I glanced back at Dee, who had lost her attitude and now had her arm back around Xavier. I'm sure it was all for my sake, but she was still hanging tight.

Nope, when I looked at all that I'd lost, I knew the answer to Xavier's question. This definitely wasn't worth the price.

23

Alexis

A week had passed since the last big blowup at my house. For once I was glad my dad was out of town. A couple of hours after my parents' last argument, I had seen him packing a bag. When I'd asked him where he was going, he'd told me he had a big meeting out of town for a few days. Peace and quiet had ruled our home for a week, and as much as I wanted my dad back, I didn't know if I was ready for the peace to come to an end. My mom had called earlier in the day to tell me to come straight home from school because my dad would be there.

As I pulled up in the driveway, I saw both my mom's and dad's cars and thought about the good times we used to have. I remembered all the times my dad would hide behind the kitchen door in the mornings, and when I would come in, he would jump from behind the door and scare me. I always knew he was there, but I pretended to be scared anyway. That was our little game that I used to look forward to every morning before he left for work. I would give anything for that kind of greeting this time, right about now.

"I'm home," I announced as I walked through our foyer.

"Up here," my dad replied through the intercom. "We're in our room. Can you come up for a second?"

I slowly began walking up the stairs. I could hear my heart pounding, and I felt sick to my stomach. So many thoughts were racing through my head. Would this be "the talk" I had been dreading? I put a brave smile on my face as I reached the door.

"Hey, Daddy. I missed you," I said as I kissed him on the cheek. "Mom, how was your day?" I asked as I sat on the chaise longue.

My mom came over, sat down next to me, and took my hand. At least she looked better than she had the last time we'd talked.

"Honey, your dad and I need to talk to you—"

I interrupted her, hoping I could prolong the conversation by telling them about my day. "I know. But first I need to tell you about my day." I didn't even have anything to tell, but suddenly I felt like I could no longer take their news.

When my dad sat down on the other side of me, I knew this was serious. "Baby girl, this is important," he said softly. "You know we love you, right?"

I nodded as my eyes began to fill up with tears.

"I'm sure you've noticed how strained things have been

between your mother and me," he continued. "We've given this a lot of thought, and we need to tell you something."

I immediately started to cry because I knew what was coming next. I could feel my breathing getting heavier. My mom had tears in her eyes as well.

Even my dad choked up, but he kept talking. "You are old enough to understand certain things now. We've tried to make this marriage work, but neither of us has been happy for a long time. We both think it is best for the entire family if we get a divorce."

"What? Best for the entire family?" I screamed. Although I'd expected the news, hearing them actually say the words was like a knife in my stomach. "How could your getting a divorce be best for the family? This isn't what's best for the family. It's what's best for you two!" I knew I was crossing the line by yelling at my parents, but I couldn't help it. I was just so upset. I swear, I wanted to scream at the top of my lungs.

"Baby, I know this is hard for you," my mom said, "but splitting up really is for the best. Your dad and I see how our fighting is affecting you. I hate what it is doing to you. We wanted to wait until you graduated, but then all of us would be miserable, and that's just not healthy."

I was in full crying mode now. As my mom tried to console me, I shrugged her hand off my shoulders. This could not be happening to me. My life had never been perfect, but this would change everything. I had so many thoughts going through my head. Had anyone told my sister yet? How was she going to take it? Who would I have to live with? Would I have to change schools? I was finding it hard to breathe at this point. All I could think about was running out the door.

"I just can't deal with this right now," I whispered. "Can I go now?" I asked with tears streaming down my face.

"Baby, are you sure you don't want to talk about how you're feeling?" my mom asked. Now she wanted to be concerned with my feelings.

"No, I don't. Not right now. I just need time by myself."

My dad put his arm around me. "Okay, sweetheart. We understand. This is a lot to process. Just know that we are here if you need to talk or have any questions."

"What would we talk about?" I cried. "You've already decided for me!"

I ran to my room, slammed the door, and threw myself onto the bed, sobbing. Never in my life had I felt so bad. A few months ago, my ex-boyfriend Jaquan, Jasmine's brother, had been killed by a neighborhood gang. I had cried a lot then, but that was nothing compared to how I felt now. This was almost like losing a loved one all over again.

I felt like my life as I knew it was coming to an end.

24

Camille

Forget all of 'em. Each and every one of my so-called friends. That's what I had been telling myself all day. Even after the way they'd dissed me at school yesterday, I'd tried to call Jasmine and make up. She'd had her bratty brothers say she was busy. Then neither Alexis nor Angel had returned my calls, even though I'd left a message.

Maya told me that before all was said and done, I would find out who my true friends were. I definitely had found out who my friends *weren't*.

"Camille, are you all right?" my mother asked, appearing in my bedroom door.

I had been standing in front of the mirror, lost in thought. I spun around and tried to fake a smile. "I'm fine."

My mother peered closer at me. "Have you been crying?"

I glanced at my reflection. My eyes were red. Probably because I *had been* crying about ten minutes ago, just before I'd told myself to suck it up and blow my friends off.

"No, I'm fine. Just my allergies," I replied.

My mother folded her arms across her chest. "Since when did you get allergies?"

I didn't want a heart-to-heart. "Mom, I'm running late." I started gathering up my stuff.

"So, are you really going to go to this party without your friends?" she asked.

"I don't have any friends," I snapped.

"Don't be ridiculous, Camille. If anything, you need to be remembering who your real friends are."

"Mom, Alexis and 'nem are not my friends. In fact, they're the biggest haters of all." I flung my purse over my shoulder.

She sighed heavily. "Somehow I seriously doubt that," she replied. "Camille, I don't think all of your friends just up and decided to one day turn on you. Think about it. It must be something you're doing."

"Why are you taking their side?" I cried.

"I'm not taking their side," my mom responded. "I just want you to look at it objectively."

"Whatever."

"And while I'm thinking about it, did that man ever say something about that video—you know, editing that trash out at the end?" My mom had called Mark several times, but he hadn't gotten back to her.

"I talked to Mark," I continued explaining. "He said he was going to try, but it might be too late and too costly to change the video, because it's already in rotation."

"That's not open for discussion, Camille," she said flatly. "And if I need to talk to him, I will. I've already talked with Mr. Canady," she said, referring to my dad's old friend, a big-time attorney in Houston.

Fear edged into my voice. "What do you mean?"

"Exactly what I said. Mr. Canady said that without my consent, you are underage and that video cannot continue to air. And that permission slip I signed was clear, there were to be no provocative images. So they need to pull it. I don't care how much it costs."

"Mom!"

"Don't 'Mom' me." Her hard stare pinned me down. "Now, I agreed to let you do this under one condition—that it be done with class and dignity. There was nothing classy or dignified about what I saw on that screen."

I was silent. I'd been lucky. So far she hadn't seen the newspaper. I knew I really should have told her about it, but I hadn't been able to get up the nerve. Plus, I knew she would totally flip out.

I didn't even feel like arguing anymore. Truth be told, I wasn't in the mood to party. More than anything, I wanted to transport myself back in time to before this stupid talent show.

She must've sensed my frustration because she finally said, "Well, I guess you should get going. Have fun. Be careful in my car."

I had my own car, a beat-up Toyota Camry that we'd just gotten fixed. But I had begged my mom to let me drive hers tonight, because I so did not want to be rolling up to this party in my hoopty. It would've been nice to drive up flossing in Alexis's BMW, but oh, well.

"'Bye," I said, stomping past her.

She reached out her arm to stop me. "I still love you," she said, kind as ever.

That melted my heart. My mom and I had been through a lot. The stress I'd caused her back when I'd gotten into all that trouble with Keith had given her a heart attack. Yeah, she'd tried to say that hadn't been the cause, but I'd known it had been. After almost losing her, I'd realized how much she meant to me. "I love you, too, Mama." I leaned over and kissed her cheek.

She took my chin. "Sweetie, I'm going to let you work this out on your own, but I'm telling you, true friends are the ones that are there for you whether you're hot . . . or not. And please understand that God is gonna work everything out. It might not be how you want it or when you want it, but God has it already figured out."

I smiled. I hoped God would go ahead and work things out—because I didn't know how much more of this drama I could take.

25

Alexis

The sight of Angelica brought a smile to my face. Especially when she pushed a large pink stuffed rabbit at me.

"Auntie Lexi! We bring Snuggles to make you feel better!"

"Ohhhhh." I took the rabbit, kissed Angelica, then stepped aside and let Angel and her daughter in.

"You two didn't have to come over," I said, shutting the door behind them.

"Please, it gave us an excuse to get out of the house." Angel set Angelica down, and she immediately raced over to start playing with my Wii. It wasn't on, but she didn't seem to care.

"I just talked to you," I said, shutting the door.

"And I told you, I don't like hearing you sound so

bummed out. So I came to hang out with you. Plus, I brought you this." She held up an *OK!* magazine. "Thought you might want to read about Paula Abdul not coming back to *American Idol.* I couldn't catch up with Jasmine and Tyeesha. So it's just me and you." Angel plopped down on the sofa.

"And me!" Angelica exclaimed.

"And you," I said, ruffling her hair. "Let me get us something to eat." Angel smiled as she tossed the magazine on the coffee table.

I made my way into the kitchen, pulled a big bag of gourmet popcorn out of the pantry, dumped it into a bowl, grabbed two sodas and made my way back into the living room. I stopped in the door and watched Angel and Angelica. Angel had turned on the Wii Cheer game. Even though Angelica wasn't doing her cheerleader right, they looked like they were having the time of their lives. It made me long for the days when my mom and I used to do fun stuff. It had been a very long time since we had, but seeing Angel and her daughter made me miss it more than ever.

"She is too cute," I said, setting the bowl on the coffee table. Angelica spotted the popcorn, threw the Wii remote down and dove in.

"Do you mind if I put the TV on cartoons for her?" Angel asked.

"Sure," I said.

Angel walked over to the TV and changed the channel. I hadn't expected them to drop by, but I was so glad they had. My mom was upstairs, where she'd been since my father left. She wouldn't admit it, but she was totally messed up about him leaving. With Sonja gone, I had just been moping around the house all day.

"So, how are you really?" Angel asked after she'd gotten Angelica settled in.

I shrugged. "I just can't believe it. I mean, what am I supposed to do without my dad?"

Angel forced a smile. "I've been okay."

"I'm sorry. I wasn't thinking." I totally forgot that Angel's dad had walked out on them when she was a little girl. Still, not belittling her situation, it was different when your dad was around, then he was suddenly gone.

"It's okay," Angel replied. "I know you're hurting."

We spent the next two hours talking about my parents, the Good Girlz, Camille and stuff at school. By the time Angel announced she had to go, I felt so much better.

"Are you sure you're gonna be okay?" she asked. She was standing in the doorway. Angelica was asleep on her shoulder. "I would stay, but I have to get Rosario her car back."

"No, you made me feel better," I said. "Thanks so much."

She smiled, gently hugging me before heading to her car.

"Who was that?" my mom asked as the door closed. I hadn't heard her come downstairs, but I could tell by her puffy eyes that she hadn't just been resting like I'd thought.

"That was Angel. She came by for a while."

My mom sat on the sofa and patted for me to come sit next to her. "I'm sorry, baby. I really shouldn't have left you to fend for yourself today."

I sat down next to her. "It's okay." I wanted to tell her I'd been getting used to it lately, but I figured now wasn't the time.

"I guess we should drive up to tell your sister tomorrow."

I thought about Sharon. Despite the expensive facility she was in, she wasn't improving the way my mother would've liked. I thought that maybe we didn't need to add to her problems—if she even understood what divorce was.

"Let's go see her," I said. "But can we hold off on telling her about . . ." I couldn't even say it out loud.

My mother stroked my hair. "You're right." She stared at me with tears in her eyes. "I know we've kind of left you to grow up on your own so fast. I'm sorry," she said. "But it's just me and you now, sweetpea."

I laid my head on her shoulder. "I hate the sound of that," I said softly.

"I do, too, baby. I do, too," my mom replied. We sat in silence for the next hour, my mom holding and comforting me like Sonja used to. I know we were both wondering how we would adjust to my father not being there. I finally decided to ask something that had been on my mind all day.

"Mom, do you think Daddy will get another family?"

She sighed heavily. "I think we just have to prepare for the worst, baby. Personally, I believe your father is married to his work. But who knows? I wouldn't be surprised if he did find someone else." She sounded more like she was talking to herself. She must've realized it, because she quickly corrected herself. "Just know that if he does, it doesn't mean that he doesn't love you. He just doesn't love me," she mumbled.

The whole idea caused her to break down sobbing again, and I felt awful about even asking. "Mom, I'm so sorry."

She sniffed. "It's not your fault." She dabbed her eyes. "I have to go lie down. I can't take this."

As I watched her leave, I was so angry that I kicked the coffee table over. My mother was hurting. I was miserable. And the idea of my father getting another family made my stomach turn.

I couldn't let that happen. I had to do whatever I could to keep it from happening. Only I had no idea what that would be.

As I fell back against the sofa, my eyes made their way to the *OK!* magazine Angel had brought over. It had fallen to the floor when I'd kicked the table. I was about to pick it up when I glanced at the front cover. In a small box next to Paula Abdul was a picture of a teary-eyed man and woman, holding a young girl. I picked the magazine up and read the headline. "Reunited After a Horrible Ordeal."

Looking at the picture of the smiling young girl, her parents hugging her tightly, made me think. For that family, the only thing that mattered was being together again. I didn't even know what had happened to the little girl, but from the looks on her parents' faces, nothing mattered except the fact that they had her back. Maybe I needed to bring my family together as well. My eyes grew wide as a thought popped into my head. "United in Tragedy," the subhead read. *That's what I needed.* I wouldn't go so far as doing anything tragic, but maybe a horrible ordeal would be just what my family needed to put us back together.

26

Camille

If inside looked anything like outside, this party was about to be off the chain. It seemed like everybody in Houston had come out to celebrate Sisco's twenty-first birthday bash.

I had just pulled into the parking lot when I spotted Maya and two other girls I didn't recognize. She waved and pointed to a spot that had just opened up on the first row. *Just my luck,* I thought as I carefully pulled into the spot. I was grateful I didn't have to search for a parking spot.

"Hey, girl," Maya said after I caught up with them.

"Hey, Maya," I replied.

"This is Toya and Tangie," she said, motioning to the girls with her. "They are friends of mine."

I smiled, wondering if the girls were in the business. I decided to ask. "Nice to meet you. Are you two dancers also?"

"Chile, please," Toya said. "We're just hanging with my girl. We grew up together," she said, pointing between herself and Maya.

I struggled to contain the confused look on my face. After all, Maya had been the main one telling me I needed to be selective with my friends and only hang out with "industry people."

"But it looks like hanging out with Maya ain't as profitable as it used to be," Tangie snapped, rolling her eyes.

Maya rolled her eyes right back. "You coulda stayed at home."

That's just what I needed—more drama. "What's up?" I asked, adjusting my rhinestone Baby Phat belt before applying some MAC lip gloss.

Maya blew a heavy breath. "Girl, can you believe they don't have my name on the VIP list? So the bouncer gon' tell me to just wait in the line." She put one hand on her hip and motioned toward the long line with her other hand. The line snaked down the sidewalk and around the corner.

"Wow," I said, taking in all the people. The party would be over by the time we made it through that line.

"Hey," Maya said, like an idea had just come to her. "What am I thinking? I know your name is on the VIP list." She grabbed my arm and led me toward the door. I felt funny marching past all of those people, most of whom were looking at us real crazy for cutting in line.

"You back?" the bouncer asked. "I told you—"

"We're here with my girl," Maya said, leaning in close to me like we were best friends since kindergarten. She tapped his clipboard. "So check your little list there and find her name. Camille . . ." She looked at me, unsure.

"Harris," I finished for her. "Camille Harris. I mean, Camille Simone," I said, remembering my stage name.

He shot Maya a skeptical look, then glanced down at his clipboard. A second later his expression changed.

"You're good," he said, stepping aside to let me in. I walked through, and Maya quickly followed. He stuck up his hand. "They wit' you?" he asked me.

I nodded, and he stepped aside.

"What?" Maya said as she sashayed past him, giving him the hand.

"That's what I'm talking about," Tangie said, all boastful now, bumping me with her hip. "I need to be hanging with you."

"Whatever, Tangie," Maya said.

The club was unlike anything I'd ever seen. The place was filled with people everywhere. Toya and Tangie quickly headed to the bar. "I know they're going to get their drink on," Maya tsked. "You want something?"

"Ummm, I guess I'll take a Coke."

"A Coke?" Maya looked at me like I was crazy.

"Yeah."

"You want some rum in that?" she asked.

My eyes grew wide. "Rum?" I had tasted some of my cousin's strawberry daiquiri one time, but I definitely had never had a drink like a rum and Coke. "Ummm, you do know I'm only seventeen, right?" I asked. Maybe she thought I was older. I didn't want to seem like a prude, but I didn't want her getting mad at me because she thought I was older than I actually was.

"And? I'm only twenty," Maya giggled. "Besides, I ain't your mama. Shoot, this is a party. We're supposed to be getting our drink on."

Suddenly I felt very uncomfortable. I mean, I knew a lot of people at my school who drank, but I wasn't one of them. I remembered this girl who had come to our school freshman year. She was badly disfigured; her face was all burned up. She'd shown us pictures of when she used to be a teenage beauty queen. One night she'd gotten behind the wheel after drinking. She'd had a horrible car crash that had left most of her body burned. Since I didn't ever want to put myself in a position like that, I stayed away from liquor. That had never been a problem, because the other Good Girlz felt the same way I did.

"Naw, I'm gonna pass," I finally said. "Just Coke."

"Suit yourself." Maya shrugged. "Me, I'm about to get my party *and* my drink on!" She snapped her fingers to the music as it thumped throughout the club.

I took a seat at a corner table. Everyone looked like they were having the time of their lives, but I couldn't help but wonder what in the world I'd gotten myself into. In a space crowded with people, I felt all alone.

That feeling didn't fade over the next hour. My new "friends" had abandoned me, and I was bored out of my mind. I'd joined Maya and Tangie for a minute, but they'd disappeared. Maya had gone off with some up-and-coming rapper, and Tangie was flirting with every man with pants on. They'd only come and found me when they hadn't been able to get into the VIP section.

Now I sat up here alone watching them party like crazy.

"Are you sure you don't want anything?" the waitress said as she came over to me again.

"No, thanks," I said, shaking my head. I'd already had three Cokes. I started thinking about what Alexis, Jasmine, Angel and even Tyeesha were doing. I just as quickly shook the thought away, though. I needed to get away from thinking about the Good Girlz. As far as I was concerned, the Good Girlz didn't exist anymore.

"So, you wanna tell me why a beautiful girl like you is sitting up here by yourself?"

I smiled as I turned to greet the person talking to me. "Hey, Sisco. I was wondering if you were coming."

"Of course I'm coming. It's my birthday party."

"I guess you're right." I laughed.

"So why aren't you dancing with your girls?" he said, motioning to Maya and Tangie, who were now standing on top of a table dancing.

"They're not really my girls," I replied, shrugging.

"Oh, I forgot," he said with an exaggerated frown, "you're one of them sweet girls. They're probably a little too fast for your taste." He licked his lips as he looked me up and down.

I smiled without responding. The last thing I wanted was to get caught up in the middle of some "he said," "she said" mess.

"Yo, B, gimme a minute," he said, motioning to the bodyguard that was always at his side.

B immediately stepped back, almost fading into the darkness.

Sisco scooted in close to me. At first my heart skipped, but then I started to feel uncomfortable. He was a little too close.

"You know, you have a beautiful voice," he said.

"Thank you."

He surprised me as he took a finger and ran it along my

thigh. "And I like this whole innocent thing about you," he said, leaning in. "You know with me being out on the road and stuff, I get tired of the groupie-type chicks."

"Oh, no, I'm definitely not a groupie." I was trying not to stiffen up under that finger.

"I know, that's why I'm feeling you." He leaned back, looked me up and down again, then said, "Not to mention, you fine as all get out."

His compliments were flattering, but the way he was looking at me was making me uneasy.

"So, how does it feel to be twenty-one?" I said, trying to get his gaze off me.

He shrugged nonchalantly. "Like it did to be twenty."

"At least you're legal now," I joked, motioning to the bottle of Moët champagne he had in his hand.

"So? I could drink this even when I wasn't legal," he said arrogantly.

I was kind of shocked, because I had always thought Sisco was one of the good guys. The more I thought about it, though, the more popular he got, the more he seemed to take on this gangsta persona. I wondered if everything he did was an act.

"Sisco, are you from around here?" I decided to steer the conversation to more neutral ground.

"Right here. Right now. That's what I want to talk about," he said, scooting closer again.

"I was just making conversation," I said, scooting away.

He closed the distance once again. "So, what you think about the video?" He moved a strand of hair out of my face. With him so close, I could smell the strong odor of liquor. He had to be pretty drunk.

"You, know, about that," I said. I had been trying to get

up the nerve to talk to him about his failure to ask Mark to delete that final scene, but I'd been too scared. Now he'd given me the perfect opening. "I thought you said you were going to talk to someone about taking out that scene."

"Did I say that?"

"Yeah, you did."

He shrugged again. "Oh, well, guess I forgot. But what's the big deal? I think the scene was hot."

"Yeah, but—"

Before I could continue, Sisco leaned in and kissed me hard. It caught me off guard, and I immediately tried to push him off me.

"What are you doing?" I asked.

"What you want me to," he said, grabbing my shirt so hard that it ripped at the neckline. "You ain't gotta play innocent with me."

I pushed him again, a lot harder. "Get off of me, boy!"

"Innocent and hard to get." He stood, violently grabbed my arm and yanked me up out of my seat. "Come on, girl, let's get out of here and go back to my place."

I jerked away. "What part of 'I'm not going with you' are you not getting?" My voice was loud, and several people turned to look at us.

He turned mean. "Look, I'm tired of you chicken head girls leading me on, then tryin' to act like you don't know what you're doin'." He grabbed me and pinned me up against the wall.

"You're hurting me," I whimpered. His hands were squeezing my arms so hard that I knew it would leave a bruise.

B finally walked over to us. "Yo, dog, you a'ight?" I was the one pinned up, so why was he trying to see if Sisco was all right?

"I'm straight," Sisco said, letting go of me.

"Well, I'm not." I was shaking, and I wanted to go home.

"Hey, you need to chill," B said. "My man don't want no drama."

"Are you for real?" I cried. "Did you just see what he did?"

Just then a security guard from the club came over. He wasn't Sisco's pal. "Miss, are you okay?"

"No," I said, glaring at Sisco. He looked like he was daring me to say something.

"Yo," B said, stepping up to the guard, "my man and his girl just had a little beef. They're good."

The guard checked with me. "Miss?"

I really wanted to say something, but everyone was standing around staring at me. They'd seen what he'd done, and they were all looking like I was the bad one.

I finally let it go. "I'm fine."

The guard hesitated.

"Man, she said she's straight," Sisco said.

The guard, still looking unsure, finally walked off.

The crowd slowly dispersed. Sisco leaned in and whispered in my ear, "You cool after all. You sure you don't wanna come back to my place?"

"Leave me alone," I muttered.

Sisco was offended, but he shrugged. "Cool. See you at the shoot tomorrow." He blew me a kiss, then turned to his bodyguard. "Yo, B, find me another freak to take home."

B immediately scurried off and left me all alone, feeling as low as I ever could imagine.

27

Camille

After Sisco left me at the club last night, Maya and Tangie came to do something I'd heard referred to as "spin control." I don't know if someone had put them up to it or if they'd just decided to do it on their own, but they immediately started trying to convince me that Sisco was drunk, he hadn't meant anything, and I needed to get some tougher skin if I wanted to make it in this business.

The thing was, I wasn't sure I even wanted to make it in this business anymore.

Maya had told me I'd be a fool to walk away, because I was going to be the hottest thing that had come out of Houston since Beyoncé. When I told her I couldn't appreciate

Sisco referring to me as a freak, she told me he hadn't meant anything by it. That was just the way he talked.

"Hey, Camille," Taraji said, walking into my dressing room. We were about to shoot a promo for the Hip Hop honors. "Look, I heard what happened last night, but you need to just let that ride. Sisco didn't mean anything. Those cameras are out there for this promotional shoot, and they're expecting to see you at Sisco's side with a smile on your face. So that's what I'm gonna need."

"But—"

"But grow up," she snapped. The sympathetic tone she'd had when she'd first walked in was gone. "This is the big leagues now. Just suck it up and keep moving."

I wanted to scream at her. When had it become okay for Sisco to be such a jerk? Was anyone going to call him on what he'd done? Somehow, I seriously doubted it.

"Look, Sisco is sorry." Taraji handed me a clipboard. "If you can just sign this, saying that you recognize it was all a big misunderstanding, he'd like to give you this." She handed me an envelope.

I slowly took it. "What's this?"

A flicker of doubt appeared in her eyes. "These papers are just, you know, because people are always trying to sue him."

I looked confused for a moment, then reached down and opened the envelope. Inside was a check for five thousand dollars. "What in the world? Are you trying to pay me off to sign those papers?"

"No," Taraji said a little too quickly. "That's your payment for today's appearance."

I stared at the check. No one had said anything about me getting paid for this appearance today. I mean, I had money coming from the actual video shoot, but I wasn't expecting that for another two weeks.

"We need to get moving," Taraji said briskly, handing me a pen. I looked back and forth between the papers and the check. Five thousand dollars was a lot of money. Maybe Maya and Tangie were right. Sisco had been drinking, and he'd just gone a little overboard.

Taraji smiled as I took the pen from her. Don't ask me why, but I felt like I was selling my soul to the devil.

I tucked my check safely away in my bag and headed to the set. Sisco arrived at the same time that I did. I half expected him to apologize, but he didn't even acknowledge me.

The photographer had just begun positioning people for the shoot when I noticed Mark, the director, huddled over in a corner, talking with some executive-looking person in a navy suit. My eyes widened in horror when I realized who else they were talking to. My mother!

"Where did this trash come from?" she shouted. I cringed when I saw what was in her hand. She was waving a copy of *Insite*, the newspaper with my photo all over the front. "My child will not be degraded like this! I know you still haven't changed that video. Let me remind you that she is not of legal age! Don't make me sue everybody up in this room!"

"Mama!" I was horrified.

At the mention of suing, the man in the navy suit turned a deep red and started nervously fidgeting with his briefcase.

"I told you I was not playing with you. You might not have called me back, but I know you got my message." My mother wagged the paper at Mark. "You get a retraction in this paper. And either they cut that crap out or the video comes off the air now!"

Sisco, who had stopped to take in the commotion, finally stomped over to them. "What's up, Mark?"

The director looked extremely flustered. "I can't deal with this. I can't deal with this," he kept repeating.

"Well, somebody's going to deal with it," my mother said.

"Look, old lady, don't come up in here on my set trippin'," Sisco said.

My mother stopped her rant and stared at him like he'd gone stone-cold crazy. " 'Old lady'?"

"Yo, you heard me."

" 'Yo'? Is that how your mama taught you to talk to someone, Crisco?" my mother hissed.

"It's Sisco," he said, not as sure of himself now.

I wanted so bad to say or do something, but I was frozen in place.

My mother wagged the paper in his face. "Let me tell you something—"

Sisco knocked the paper away. "Somebody better get this b—" Before he could finish his sentence, my mother had taken her purse and swung it as hard as she could, knocking Sisco upside the head.

"I know you were not about to fix your lips to call me out of my name, you disrespectful little ingrate!" She continued to pummel him with her oversized purse.

I stood there, dumbfounded, not believing the scene that was unfolding in front of me.

Sisco, who was acting tough a minute ago, was covering his head and screaming, "Stop! Get her off me!"

His boys, who usually had his back, were cracking up laughing. Even B, the bodyguard, was laughing.

"All y'all disrespectful," my mother said, finally stopping

her attack. "You think you're going to corrupt my child? Not as long as there's breath in my body!"

"Mrs. Harris, will you calm down?" the navy suit–wearing man said.

"No, I will not calm down." Her chest heaved up and down as she tried to catch her breath.

"This is ridiculous," Taraji said, finally speaking up. She spun toward Mark. "I told you all getting some high school girl was a bad idea, and look at all the drama we've had since we brought her on board."

I was shocked, because my mother never got this worked up about anything. But I guess the video, the tabloid, and now being disrespected by Sisco had pushed her over the edge.

"Camille, get your stuff and let's go," she demanded.

"But, Mama—"

"Did that sound like a request to you?" she snapped. "Now I hadn't planned on acting a fool, but this little ingrate wants to call me outta my name." She glared at Sisco and held up her bag in warning. "Whew, you lucky I know Jesus, or else I'd be sending you to meet Him."

"Camille, I think it's best if you leave," Taraji said. "For good."

Sisco had pulled himself together and was now looking like he wanted to punch someone. As everyone stared at me and my mom, I thought about all that I had sacrificed. I'd lost my dignity, my boyfriend and my friends. And for what?

"You know what, Taraji?" I finally said. "I couldn't agree with you more. I do need to leave." I headed out the door after my mother.

28

Alexis

Everything inside me told me this wasn't the answer. But at this point I didn't know what else to do. When Angel was pregnant, she ran away from home because her mother was planning on giving Angelica up for adoption. The road trip to find Angel had landed us all in a bunch of trouble. But she'd returned safe and sound, and her mom had ended up not giving the baby up for adoption. So, if you really thought about it, her plan had worked. That's why I couldn't help but think that maybe, just maybe, if my mom and dad freaked out about me coming up missing, they'd see that breaking up was not the answer.

I called Tyeesha to leave her a message, since neither Jasmine nor Angel had cell phones. I didn't want them worrying about me.

"Hey, Tyeesha, it's Alexis. I need you to tell Jasmine and Angel not to worry. I'm okay. You guys will just have to trust me. Hopefully, I can explain everything later." I hung up and began putting my plan into action.

I'd worked everything out. I had called my old friends from St. Pius, twins by the name of Mari and Marlee. They'd graduated last year, but they were the only ones I still kept in touch with. They were going to meet me at the Galleria Mall.

I had driven my car to the mall. I was going to leave it in the parking garage. That way it would blend in with the rest of the cars. I didn't want to have someone spot it and call the police or something.

After parking, I made my way inside the mall. I was supposed to meet the twins in front of Starbucks at two o'clock. Of course, they were late, so I killed time by window shopping in nearby stores. Once I spotted someone I knew from high school, and I turned so she wouldn't see me.

About two forty-five, the twins came bouncing toward me, their arms filled with bags. "Hey, Alexis," they sang, giving me their signature air kiss. Both of them wore all white and looked like they'd just come from a tennis match. With their bouncy blond curls, they looked like they should be doing a shampoo commercial.

"Long time, no see," Mari said.

"We've missed hanging out with you," Marlee added.

Sometimes Mari and Marlee were more trouble than they were worth, and I had all but kicked them to the curb when I'd started hanging with the Good Girlz.

"Yeah, I know. I'm sorry. But thanks for doing this," I replied.

I'd already given them the rundown on what I was doing. I'd told them I was basically running away from home to teach my parents a lesson, so I needed to stay with them for a few days. Their parents were divorced, their mother traveled all the time, and so they were basically on their own. They'd graduated from high school last year, but neither one seemed in a hurry to figure out what she was going to do with the rest of her life.

"This is so cool," Marlee said excitedly.

I groaned at their giddiness. Maybe I should've really run away. But I was too much of a scaredy cat to make it out somewhere on my own, especially after what had happened when we'd tried to find Angel. Some creepy guys had chased us down an abandoned dirt road. We'd gotten away, but not before being scared out of our minds.

Nope, chillin' at the twins' house was about as far as I was going to run. And I wasn't planning on staying long. Just long enough for my mom and dad to get worked into a frenzy.

"Why are you guys late?" I asked.

"Oh, my God. Nordstrom's had a sale, like out of this world," Marlee squealed. "Look at these Prada shoes." She pulled a pair of black wedge sandals from one of the bags. "They were forty percent off."

Both girls high-fived each other. They were probably five times richer than me, but something about finding designer stuff on sale gave them a rush. I took a look at the shoes and shook my head. Even at the sale price, the shoes were still four hundred and seventy dollars.

"Let's go," I said. "Please?"

"Okay. Here, put this on," Mari said, pulling a long Hannah Montana wig and a big hat out of one of the bags.

"What is that?" I asked.

"It's your disguise." Marlee giggled. "If we're going to do this, we need to do it right."

This was too stupid for words. "Why would I need a disguise?"

"Duh? Because you're hiding, remember?" Marlee replied.

"I'm hiding from my parents. And trust me, they're not hanging out at the mall." My mom did most of her shopping in New York and Paris boutiques, and my father had all of his stuff made. He wouldn't be caught dead at the mall.

"But what if there are surveillance cameras?" Mari asked.

"Maybe in the parking lot, but I doubt they have surveillance cameras at Starbucks," I said, wondering why we were standing in the middle of the mall arguing about this.

"Well, someone may see you walking to the car with us." Mari had a look of exasperation, like she couldn't understand why I was giving her a hard time.

"By the time they sift through the videotapes, I'll be back home," I said.

"You are no fun," Marlee pouted.

I had to once again ask myself what I had gotten into. This was not a game, but they were acting like we were on some kind of scavenger hunt.

"Well, at least wear the hat. It's so cute. Another sale," Marlee sang.

"Okay, fine, whatever." I took the hat and put it on my head. "Can we go now?"

"Yes," they giggled and led the way outside to the parking garage.

After Marlee took me up one row of cars and down another, we walked back to the front of the Galleria, where she told me they'd valet parked.

"So, what was the wandering through the parking garage for?" I asked.

"Surveillance cameras," Mari sang.

I just groaned and waited for the valet to bring their Range Rover around.

They giggled and talked about useless stuff all the way to their River Oaks mansion. Yet hiding out at home didn't work much for them. Before long they had lost interest.

"I'm bored," Marlee said after we watched back-to-back episodes of *Making the Band 4*.

"Me, too," Mari echoed. "Let's go to the club."

I had gotten into so much trouble the last time I'd gone to a club with the twins. They'd popped some pills—something I'd had no idea that they did—and Marlee had ended up passing out. It had been one of the most frightening things I had ever experienced.

"Ummm, that would be no," I said. "We're hiding out, remember?"

"You're hiding out, dang," Marlee said. "I'm bored. How long has it been?"

I glanced down at my watch. "Three hours," I said in exasperation.

"God, it feels like three days," she said as she fell back on the sofa.

"Look, my dad was supposed to have picked me up an hour ago, so by now they're blowing up my phone and they probably just think I'm late."

"Maybe we should call the TV stations and tell them to

put out an Amber Alert," she said, referring to the statewide notification system when a child has been abducted.

"Number one, I haven't been abducted," I said. "Number two, someone has to have seen you get kidnapped for them to do an Amber Alert."

"Hey, I can call Damien," Marlee said, talking about her wannabe thug boyfriend. The only problem was, it was kind of hard to be a thug when your parents owned six McDonald's.

"He might know someone that can fake-abduct you," she said.

"No," I replied, stopping her. "I'm not going through all of that. I'm not trying to get on the news. I'm not trying to scare my parents any more than I have to. I just want them to freak out enough to realize this whole splitting-up thing is a big mistake."

Marlee stuck out her bottom lip. "How do you know they're gonna even call the cops? It could be three or four days."

"Yeah, that's how long it would take for our parents to notice we were really gone," Mari echoed. "They'd just think we were off somewhere with our friends."

They burst out laughing like it was funny. I stared at them both in disbelief. This situation was actually quite sad. Yet anyone on the outside looking in would see us, three rich girls, and think we had it going on.

"You guys can do what you want," I finally said. "But if it's okay with you, I'm just going to stay here and chill out."

"What about tomorrow? Are you going to school?" Mari asked. "We have to teach our Pilates class tomorrow at four. Do you wanna come?"

I sighed. "I've run away," I said slowly, so they could grasp it. "No, I'm not going to school. I don't want to go to Pilates.

I'm just staying here." At this point I wanted them to go out just so I could get some peace and quiet. If I had to put up with this all night long, I would lose my mind. "You guys go out and have some fun."

"Okay," Marlee said, jumping up. "It's ladies' night at the Polo Club."

"So are we really going to leave her here?" Mari asked, standing to follow her sister.

"She said for us to go on and go."

"Yes, please go," I repeated, with a little more force than I had intended.

"Well, I'm going to go take a shower," Mari said.

Yeah, I needed them gone so I could think.

They both bounced upstairs, and I leaned back. This plan had to work. It had to bring my family back together. If it didn't, I didn't know what else I was going to do.

29

Camille

This could totally not be happening to me. I could only wonder what I had done to deserve this. I stared at the front page of the tabloid. There it was, big as day—a photo of my mom hitting Sisco with her purse. I wanted to die.

I'd arrived at school to find it taped to my locker. I quickly tore it down and spotted Dee standing at the end of my row, laughing hysterically with her friends. I so couldn't stand her!

"The chance of a lifetime and you blow it," she said, shaking her head. "Then your crazy mama attacks him."

"Go away, Dee," I replied, tossing the paper into the big steel trash can.

"That article said you're accusing Sisco of attacking you. *As if.*" She looked disgusted.

"You don't know what you're talking about."

She walked toward me, gloating. "All I know is Sisco can have any girl he wants. Trust, he doesn't have to attack some ol' stuck-up pretend-diva."

If this girl knew what was good for her, she'd get out of my face, because God knew, I was at my breaking point.

"Of course, when there are all kinds of willing skanks with no self-respect, you'd think Sisco wouldn't *need* to try and attack anyone," I said as casually as I could.

"Self-respect?" She laughed. "Letting him feel you all up, kiss all over you in front of your so-called boyfriend, call you outta your name? Oh yeah, that's *real* respectful. If anything, he thought you were a skank because you dang sure acted like one."

Usually, I would've come right back at her. But although I would never admit it, she was right. Miss Rachel was right. My mom was right. I'd put myself out there to be disrespected, and that's exactly what Sisco had done.

"Look, I'm telling you for the last time, leave me alone," I finally said.

"I just don't believe it," she went on, like I hadn't said anything. "First, you mess things up with Xavier, the hottest dude at school. But don't worry, I got that on lock now." She smiled when she said that. "Then you mess up the chance of a lifetime with Sisco."

I couldn't believe I was letting her go off on me, but I felt so dejected that I didn't have the energy to fight back.

"Dee, leave me alone," I repeated, slamming my locker shut.

She followed me. "No, I won't. I don't care what kind of star you *think* you are. You—"

"You heard her, she said leave her alone."

I never thought I'd be so happy to hear Jasmine's voice. She was standing behind Dee—or should I say, towering behind Dee. True, Jasmine had put her fighting ways behind her, for the most part anyway, but she still could strike fear in the best of them.

Dee looked Jasmine up and down like she was debating whether or not to say something. I guess she decided she didn't want to get her pretty face damaged, because she threw up her hands.

"Whatever. I'm done talking to this freak anyway. I gotta go. My boo Xavier wants to meet me for lunch," she said, waltzing off.

It took everything in my power not to cry. "Th—thanks, Jasmine," I managed to say after Dee left. "It means a lot that you would do that for me."

Jasmine turned away and punched in the code to her locker, which was right next to mine. "It ain't about you, because, after all, we're not your friends." She threw her backpack in her locker, slammed it closed, then looked at me. "You made it clear who your real friends were. So, next time, get them to have your back. Because I'm done."

The firmness in her voice told me that this time, Jasmine meant it.

30

Camille

After Jasmine left, my head started pounding. I'd wanted to stay home from school today, but I had a midterm exam that I couldn't miss.

"Miss Harris, I know you're a superstar and all, but take the sunglasses off in my hallway," said our principal, Mrs. Lexington.

I removed my glasses and stuffed them down into my book bag. The funny thing was, I wasn't trying to be a diva. I just had the glasses on because I had a headache and the light was hurting my eyes.

My heart skipped when I saw Jasmine had stopped at the end of the hall to talk to Angel. As our eyes met, I wondered if I should go over and say something, apologize, anything to get us back on the right track. But before I could make up my mind, Jasmine rolled her eyes and walked off again.

While Angel didn't roll her eyes, she did turn and follow Jasmine.

"Whatever," I mumbled as I walked to my class.

I'd just taken a seat at the front of the classroom when Xavier walked in with Dee. He had his arm draped around her shoulder.

I fought back tears as I noticed she was wearing his letterman jacket.

I tried to tell myself it was all for show because he knew I would be in this class. I tried my best not to notice them. At least he tried to drop his arm. Dee, on the other hand, was straight putting on a show, talking about "baby, this" and "baby that." I buried my head in my book and didn't look up.

Class had gotten under way when Mrs. Lexington came into the room. She whispered something to Mrs. Williams, our teacher, who then shook her head. Then they both lined me up in their sights. *Oh, God, what was I getting in trouble for now?*

"Camille, Mrs. Lexington would like to speak with you in her office," Mrs. Williams announced.

Chatter immediately filled the classroom.

"They're probably arresting her for making false accusations against Sisco," this girl in the back of the class said.

I ignored her as I eased out of my seat.

"Oh, and please take your stuff," Mrs. Williams added.

The "ooohs" grew louder, because if I was taking my stuff, that meant I wasn't coming back and was probably in big trouble.

"What now?" I groaned. I followed Mrs. Lexington out of

the class and down the hall, trying my best to keep up. Her heels clicked smartly down the hallway as she speed-walked back to her office.

"What's going on?" I asked.

She didn't reply. Instead, she simply opened her office door and motioned for me to go first.

As soon as I walked in, I spotted Alexis's mother. She was sitting in a chair in front of Mrs. Lexington's desk, softly sobbing. Alexis's father stood over her, his hand on her shoulder. His eyes were puffy, like he'd been crying, too.

"Hi, Mr. and Mrs. Lansing," I said apprehensively.

Mrs. Lansing immediately jumped up and raced over to me. "Please tell me you've seen her! You know where she is?" She clutched my jacket like she was hanging on for dear life. It was actually kinda scary.

"Huh?" I stammered. "What are you talking about? Seen who?"

"Camille, we asked you to come because we need to know if you have seen or talked to Alexis," Mrs. Lexington said.

"Ummm, no," I said. I started to tell them that we were no longer friends, but I decided against it. "I mean, I have second period with her, but she wasn't there today." All of a sudden my heart started racing. Now that I thought about it, her being absent was weird. Alexis hadn't missed a single day of school since she'd transferred to Madison. "Did something happen to Alexis?"

As soon as I said that, Alexis's mother started sobbing even louder.

"Come on, Veronique. You have to hold it together," Mr. Lansing said, helping her back down into her seat.

"Is something going on with Alexis?" I repeated.

"Camille, we need you to be honest," Mrs. Lexington continued. "If you know where Alexis is, we need you to please tell us."

"No, I don't."

"We've asked Jasmine and Angel to come in as well," she said, warning me. "I know you all are very close, and you may think you're looking out for Alexis, but lying for her is not in her best interests."

No sooner had she mentioned their names than Angel and Jasmine appeared in the doorway, looking just as confused as me.

"Girls, please come on in," Mrs. Lexington said.

"Please tell me one of you knows where Alexis is," Mrs. Lansing said before they could even enter.

Both of them exchanged looks that said they didn't know anything.

"She's not in school today?" Angel asked.

Alexis's mom buried her head in her hands again.

"No, she's missing," Alexis's father said. "We think someone may have abducted her."

"What?" all three of us said at the same time.

Her father sighed heavily. "They found her car at the Galleria Mall. It was parked in the garage. A security guard ran the plate because it sat there overnight. They also found her cell phone on the ground next to the car, and I know my daughter never goes anywhere without her cell phone. So we think something may have happened."

"Arthur is calling in favors because the police are saying she has to be missing forty-eight hours," her mother added. "But in the meantime, we were hoping you girls could help us."

Alexis's father was about to say something else when the phone rang. He pulled it out of his jacket pocket and looked at the caller ID. "Excuse me, this is the police."

"Mrs. Lansing, do you all think something happened to Alexis?" I asked after her husband had stepped outside.

"We don't know," she cried. "God, please don't let anything happen to my baby."

When Alexis's father returned, he looked visibly irritated. "This is ridiculous," he snapped. "The police want to know if it's possible that she would run away."

"What?" her mother sniffed. "Did you tell them, of course not?"

"Of course I did." He ran his hands through his hair as he paced back and forth. "Alexis has no reason to run away." He sounded like he was choking back a lump in his throat. "But at this point I don't care why she's gone. I just want her back."

It was heartbreaking to see Alexis's parents so upset—especially because they had been two of the most together people I knew.

Watching them, I became determined. I didn't know how, but I was going to do whatever it took to find out what had happened to Alexis. I just hoped that nothing bad had happened. If I ever got a chance to see my friend again, I vowed, I would never again mess our friendship up.

31

Camille

"Guys, what are we gonna do?" I was standing outside the front office with Angel and Jasmine. The bell had just rung and students had started scattering everywhere.

The two of them looked at me, then turned back to each other, basically ignoring me.

"I say we catch up with Tyeesha and get her to come help us look for Alexis," Jasmine said to Angel. It was obvious she wasn't trying to include me in anything. They hadn't even spoken to me since they'd set foot in the office.

"Look, I know you guys are mad at me right now," I began.

"That's the understatement of the year," Jasmine cracked.

Now wasn't the time to be fighting with Jasmine, so I just said, "Well, you can be mad all you want—*after* we find

Alexis." They both had this look on their faces like they knew I was right, but neither wanted to admit it.

I took advantage of their silence. "Do you think someone abducted her?"

"I have a feeling she ran away," Jasmine said.

"Are you serious?" I asked. "Why would she run away?"

Jasmine didn't answer, but Angel said, "Probably because of everything that's going on with her mom and dad."

"What's going on with her parents?" I asked. Suddenly, I felt horrible. Here I was, so concerned with this stupid video, that I hadn't realized my best friend was in trouble.

"You know, it's really sad that you don't even know," Jasmine said with disgust.

"Would you just tell me what's going on?" I asked.

"Alexis's parents are getting a divorce, and she's totally messed up over it," Angel said.

"What?" I exclaimed.

"Yeah. If you weren't so wrapped up in your fame, you would have known that." Jasmine glared at me.

I tried to think. "Yeah, she mentioned it. But I thought she was just exaggerating."

"No, Camille, she's dead serious," Jasmine snapped. "And no, I don't understand it, because where I'm from, people get divorced every single day and it doesn't faze the kids. But that's not Alexis's world. Her parents' staying together meant the world to her, and the bottom line is, we were there for her and you weren't."

Of course, that brought tears to my eyes.

"Come on, Jasmine, calm down," Angel said. "Yes, we were there for her, but in the end, it didn't really matter, did it? She's still gone."

Jasmine folded her arms in defiance.

"Hey, you guys," Tyeesha said, walking up to us. "I've been looking for y'all. I just got this strange message that Alexis left on my phone yesterday. It said for us not to worry and just trust her."

"I knew it!" Jasmine exclaimed. "She did run away."

"What? What's going on?" Tyeesha asked. Jasmine and Angel immediately started filling her in. I couldn't help but feel a tinge of jealousy. It's like Tyeesha had really taken my place, and I had no one to blame but myself.

" . . . and now Camille wants to come in here, acting all concerned."

"Okay, Jasmine, don't go off on me," Tyeesha said. "Now's not the time for that. Let's focus all our energy on trying to figure out where Alexis is."

I was so glad Tyeesha was being the voice of reason. Like it or not, they needed me to help.

"Okay, so tell me, does she talk to any of her old friends?" Tyeesha asked.

"No, we're all she really hangs out with," Jasmine said.

I snapped my fingers as I remembered someone. "Hey, what about those girls she got into trouble with at the nightclub that time? I think they were twins. They went to school with her at St. Pius."

"Oh, yeah," Angel said, nodding. "They were like stupid rich kids. Alexis did used to hang with them a lot before she met us. But how are we supposed to find them?"

"It shouldn't be that hard to get information on some rich twins that go to St. Pius. So let's go," I said.

Jasmine wasn't taking orders from me. "How are we going anywhere? Alexis is the one with the car."

"Dang, I can try to track down my sister and see if we can use her car," Angel replied.

Jasmine's brow creased with worry. "There's no telling how long that will take."

"Hey, I have my car," I said. "I just got it fixed."

Jasmine let out a long sigh, like she wished there had been some other option.

"Well, then, cool, let's go," Tyeesha said before Jasmine could protest.

I could tell Jasmine wasn't feeling the idea. Angel must've seen it in her face as well, because she said, "Jas, we have to find Alexis."

"Fine, whatever." She shrugged as she started walking toward the student parking lot. "But I'm sitting in the back."

I didn't say anything as I led them to my car. Yes, Jasmine was being a bit extreme, but I guess I deserved her cold shoulder.

We headed to St. Pius. Luckily, we'd gone there a couple of times with Alexis, so we knew where the school was located. We were just worried because it was after four. Since school was out, we didn't know if anyone would be around to help us.

"Good, we're in luck," I said as we pulled up in front of the school. "The cheerleaders are still here."

I eased into the no parking zone at the front of the school, and we all jumped out of the car. The cheerleaders stopped in mid-chant and stared at us racing toward them. The looks on their faces told us we weren't exactly being welcomed with open arms.

"Sorry to disturb your practice," Jasmine said, "but we

were wondering if you guys know a girl named Alexis Lansing."

They looked at each other before the tallest girl in the group responded. "Yeah, she used to go here. Why?"

"Have you all seen her?" I asked.

"No, we haven't seen her since she transferred," the tall girl answered.

"Didn't she like transfer to some hood school?" a red-haired girl standing next to her said.

"Yes, can you believe it? Left St. Pius to go to some school in the hood," some girl in the back chirped.

"Maybe it was her way of trying to get in touch with her people." That came from the only black girl on the squad. I don't know if she was trying to be funny, but she looked real stupid.

I was worried that Jasmine would say something to her, but luckily, she stayed focused.

"Look, we're just trying to find out if anyone has seen her," Jasmine said.

"What about the twins?" I asked. "They go here and they're supposed to be rich."

"Everyone who goes here is rich," the tall girl said, not bothering to hide her arrogance.

"They're friends with Alexis," Angel added. "They used to hang out with her before Alexis left St. Pius."

"Oh, you mean Marlee and Mari," one of the girls said.

The tall girl elbowed her. "Look, we don't know you guys from paint," she snapped.

"We're friends of Alexis's, and she's missing. We really need to find her, and we think the twins may know where she is," Angel said.

"Well, we don't know you, and for all we know, you could be trying to kidnap or jack them," the tall girl snidely remarked.

"Girl, I don't need to jack anybody," Jasmine said, taking a step toward her.

"Jasmine . . ." Tyeesha reached out and took Jasmine's arm.

"Naw, Tyeesha. They got me messed up," Jasmine said, snatching her arm away.

"*Tyeesha*," the tall girl said, looking at the other cheerleaders before bursting out in laughter. "And let me guess, your name is Uniqua, Dominiqua and Hermalinda," she said, pointing at each of us.

"Okay, they are so asking for a beat down," Jasmine warned.

"Guys, let's go," I said. "Forget it, they're not gonna help us." I gave them a scornful look. "I saw some people on the football field. Let's go over there."

I gave them one last disgusted look before walking off. We'd just reached the car when the black cheerleader came running toward us.

"Hey," she said, "look, sorry, we get a little carried away sometimes."

None of us responded.

"Well, anyway," she continued, "Marlee and Mari graduated last year. But they teach a Pilates class from four to five at 24 Hour Fitness on Westheimer."

Bingo, we'd hit the jackpot. "Thank you," I said as we got back in the car. She raced back over to her squad mates, who didn't seem at all happy that she had come and talked to us.

"So," I asked, firing up the engine, "anybody need to work out?"

32

Camille

Anticipation filled the car. None of us knew what we would do if we couldn't find the twins, or, worse, if they didn't know where Alexis was either.

Once we pulled up in front of the gym, we just kinda stared, as if to say, *What now?*

"Should we go in and ask them if they've seen Alexis?" Angel finally said.

"No," Jasmine replied. "Because if they're anything like those girls we just left, they're not going to tell us anything."

"Okay," I said. "Let me go inside and just make sure they're here." Everyone seemed okay with that idea, and I left the car running as I headed inside.

"Excuse me, where's your Pilates class?" I asked the perky

young girl behind the front desk. She seemed like she was deep in a phone conversation, but she moved her cell away from her ear.

"Right there," she said, pointing at a large room on the side of the gym. "Are you a member?"

"Actually, I'm here to see the twins," I said.

"Oh, okay, go on back." She turned her attention back to her phone call, and I made my way over to the Pilates room.

I peeped in the window just as the twins were dismissing the class. I recognized them immediately from the few times I'd met them.

I hurried back out to the car. "I saw them," I said, jumping back into the front seat. "It looks like they're wrapping up."

Sure enough, two bubbly, perfectly tanned girls came bouncing out a few minutes later. They were laughing as they climbed into a white Range Rover.

"What if they aren't going home?" Angel asked as I pulled out to follow them.

"We follow them until they do," Jasmine replied.

They drove for ten minutes before pulling into the drive-thru at Starbucks. We waited patiently until they pulled back onto the access road. We followed them for ten more minutes, when they pulled into a residential area.

"Oh, no," I groaned when I noticed the huge wrought-iron gate in front of their massive house. "Now what?"

We sat for a moment before Tyeesha pointed. "Now we go in." The twins had driven into their driveway and left the gate open.

"These girls are a disaster waiting to happen," I said. Not only had they not paid any attention to the fact that they were being followed but they'd also left the gate wide open for anyone to come in.

I pulled into the driveway. I had barely turned off the car when one of the twins swung the front door to the house open. Her sister was right behind her.

They were standing there in matching outfits looking like Thing One and Thing Two.

"May we help you?" Thing One said.

"Yeah, we already gave to the homeless," Thing Two added. Then they giggled like they had said something really funny.

I ignored their sarcasm. "We are friends of Alexis Lansing. Have you guys seen her?"

They looked at each other, faking confused expressions. "Mari, do you know anyone named Alexis?"

"No, Marlee, I don't."

"Sorry, can't help you." Marlee shrugged. It was so obvious they were lying.

"She's lying," I said, deciding to call her on it. "I can see it in her eyes."

Marlee raised her right eyebrow. "Sweetie, the only thing you see in my eyes is thirteen-hundred-dollar Lasik surgery."

Okay, I thought the girls at their school were bad. These chicks took the cake.

"How 'bout we call the cops and ask them to ask you where Alexis is?"

"How 'bout we call the cops and ask them to have you escorted off our property?" Mari replied. "You're trespassing."

"Forget this," Jasmine muttered, peering over their shoulders. "Alexis!" she yelled. "Are you in there?"

"Excuse me, hel-lo. This is not Cuney Homes," Mari said, referring to a housing project.

I started to respond when I looked up and saw the blinds in an upstairs window quickly close. "Someone's up there," I said, pointing.

"Move," Jasmine said, pushing Mari aside so hard that she fell down.

"Marlee, call nine one one!" Mari screamed.

"Alexis!" Jasmine yelled again.

"Are you all kidnapping her?" Angel asked.

Mari pulled herself up off the ground. "We don't have to kidnap anyone. Alexis is here on her own free will."

Marlee looked at her sister and groaned.

"Oops," Mari said, her hand going to her mouth.

Jasmine shook her head at them as she bogarted her way inside. We quickly followed her.

"Alexis!" Jasmine called out. "Everybody's worried sick! Where are you?"

As soon as we stepped inside the gigantic foyer, Alexis appeared at the top of the stairs. "Would you guys chill with all the noise?" she said, making her way down the stairs.

I had never been so relieved to see someone. We all ran over and hugged her.

"Girl, you had us scared to death!" Jasmine pushed her shoulder. "Don't you ever do that again."

"Yeah, Alexis, why would you do that?" Angel added. "You know that girl from our school came up missing after running away. They found her body. I was scared that might have happened to you."

Alexis looked worn out, like she hadn't slept for the last few days. Her hair was pulled back in a scrappy-looking ponytail, and she wore a pair of gray sweats.

Mari and Marlee were standing behind us looking like two pit bulls. "Hey guys. Gimme a minute," Alexis said to them.

They shot us hateful looks before spinning and leaving the room.

Alexis sighed, her face filled with regret. "I know, I wasn't thinking. You guys don't understand everything that's been going on in my house. I just needed to do something."

"And you thought this was the answer?" Tyeesha said. "We talked about this."

"I guess I wasn't thinking." She lowered her head.

"Well, get your stuff and let's go," Jasmine demanded.

"I don't have any stuff, and I'm not going anywhere," Alexis said, making us do a double-take. "And if you all are my true friends, you won't tell anyone you found me."

"Come on, Alexis, don't ask us to do that," I said.

Alexis rolled her eyes at me. "Trust, I'm not asking you to do anything. Why are you even here?"

That stung, but Jasmine, of all people, came to my defense. "She's here because we were all worried about you. But don't ask any of us to do that. You know you're our girl and all, and we always got your back, but we cannot help you hide out. That's major."

"Do you know your parents were at the school? I've never seen your mother as messed up as she was," Angel added. "Every time I've ever seen her, she's been classy and together. She didn't even have on any makeup."

"What?" Alexis asked in disbelief. "My mom came out with no makeup on?"

"Exactly," Jasmine said. "Even your dad looked like he'd been crying."

She hesitated before saying, "Well, maybe this means my plan is working."

"What plan is this, Alexis?" Tyeesha asked.

"I don't know, I just kinda want them to bond in their grief or something," she said. That had to be the stupidest thing I'd ever heard, but I remembered hearing Jasmine say that while Alexis's actions might not make sense to the rest of us, they did to Alexis.

"How long do you think that will last? And why would you want them to stay together if they're unhappy?" Tyeesha asked. "I told you, it may not seem that way, but sometimes it's better if parents break up. You said yourself you were tired of the fighting. If they stayed because of some sort of bond, sooner or later their true feelings would come out and they would just start fighting again. You don't want that." Dang, that girl was good. I made a mental note to give Tyeesha a chance—that is, if they would give me another chance.

"I know your heart was in the right place," Tyeesha continued. "But at best, this will just delay the divorce process. At worst, things at home will be even more miserable than before."

Alexis sighed. "You know, I am ready to go home. I heard what everyone was saying, but my heart wouldn't let me accept it. I have to talk to my parents one last time, just to make sure they are really getting divorced."

I could tell if the divorce happened Alexis was definitely going to need her friends. And I planned to be there, whether she wanted me to be or not.

33

Alexis

I couldn't help it. I knew I had scared my parents half to death, but watching them in Miss Rachel's office right now, my father's hand resting on my mother's shoulder, gently massaging her aching muscles, brought a smile to my face. He used to do that all the time when I was little. It was his way of calming her down.

"Why are you standing here at the door?" Miss Rachel asked, walking up behind me. Camille had called her as soon as we'd left the twins' place. Miss Rachel had gotten in touch with my parents, who'd shot straight over to meet me here.

I was sure Miss Rachel was going to start lecturing me.

"Don't look at me like that," she told me. "We're going

to have a long talk, but right now you need to get in there to your parents." She motioned toward her office door.

I nodded, then eased the door open. My friends were waiting in the church sanctuary, like they were scared I'd take off if they left me alone. Camille claimed they just wanted to make sure I reunited with my parents, but whatever.

I had barely stuck my head in when my mother jumped out of her chair and raced over toward me. "Lexi! Oh, my God. I was so worried."

"Alexis!" My father was right behind her. They both squeezed me so hard I thought I would snap in half. "Oh, baby, I am so happy to see you."

"Where were you? What happened?" my mother fired at me while she grabbed my chin and examined my face. "Did anyone hurt you? They didn't tell us anything except that you'd been found. Please tell me you weren't hurt."

"I'm okay," I said, relishing the closeness.

"What happened? Where have you been?" my father asked. Surprisingly, he didn't sound mad, like I'd wasted his precious time. He just sounded relieved.

Miss Rachel was standing behind us. When I heard her clear her throat, I knew all this happy-go-lucky family stuff was about to come to an end.

"Mr. and Mrs. Lansing, if we could please have a seat," she said, pointing at the chairs in front of her desk.

My mother eased back over to the chair, never letting go of my hand.

Miss Rachel took a seat as well. "Alexis has asked me to stay here while she talks to you two. She has something she wants to say."

Both of my parents immediately turned to me with perplexed expressions.

I tried to open my mouth and say something, but nothing would come out.

Finally, Miss Rachel spoke up again. "Alexis, how about I begin?" Her voice took on a gentle tone as she turned to my parents. "Alexis ran away."

"What?" both of my parents exclaimed.

"Ran away?" my father said, confused. "You have the best of everything. Why in the world would you run away?"

The fact that he'd even had to ask that question was proof of just how out of touch my parents were.

"Yes, Lexi. Don't we give you everything? Why in the world would you even think about running away?" my mother said.

"Are you serious?" I asked, not trying to hide my irritation. That warm and fuzzy feeling I had a minute ago was definitely gone.

"Alexis, you will not be disrespectful," Miss Rachel chastised.

I bit my bottom lip. "I'm sorry. I'm not trying to be," I replied. "I just don't understand how you guys can think I'm happy."

"Because you have things most people your age only dream about," my father said.

"Do I? Yes, I have a BMW, and the finest clothes, and a credit card. But I would give it all up to get my parents to love me."

"That is absurd," my mother said, shocked. "Of course we love you."

"No, you don't. Not only do you never have time for me, but if you loved me, you'd figure out how to work things out and not get divorced!" I knew I sounded like a baby, and I knew plenty of people whose parents were divorced, but I wasn't plenty of people. Since my sister had left, my mom and dad were the only family I had. If they broke up, they'd just pawn me back and forth. At least Mari and Marlee had each other. I wouldn't have anyone.

My mother's eyes watered up. I expected her to begin one of her dramatic performances, but instead she just said, "Lexi, darling, I promise you, your father and I divorcing has nothing at all to do with you. It's us. But it doesn't diminish our love for you."

My father kneeled in front of me. "Alexis, I know we haven't been perfect parents, but if anything, this divorce has made us even more committed to making sure you get your time."

"But Marlee and Mari said their dad ran off and married some woman half his age," I responded. "She doesn't like them, so they never even see him anymore. He chose his new life over them."

"Those twins that you used to be friends with? Are they the ones that put this crazy idea in your head?" I didn't answer as my father continued talking. "Alexis, you don't ever have to worry about that."

"Sweetie, the only thing your daddy is married to is his work," my mother said, not missing a chance to get in a dig at my father.

He ignored it. "Trust me, Alexis, I have no intention of marrying someone else, and if that ever happens, she would have to understand that me and you, we're a package deal."

The idea of him marrying someone else startled both me and my mom, because she shot him a wild-eyed look. I didn't want them to start fighting, so I quickly said, "Why can't you two just stay together?"

"We don't love each other anymore," my father said matter-of-factly.

"No." I didn't want to hear that, even if it was true. "I saw you two before I came in here. You were massaging her shoulder like you used to!"

"I know that calms her down," he explained. "I still care about your mother, and I always will."

"Lexi, is that why you ran away?" my mother asked. "Because you thought it would bring us back together?"

I sighed. It sounded so stupid now. But I hadn't been thinking straight. I'd just wanted to make them stay together.

"I just thought, you know, worrying about me might bring you two closer together."

My mother shook her head in exasperation. "Lexi . . ."

"Baby, that was not the answer," my father said.

"I know." I stood up, feeling defeated. "Can we go home now?" So much for my plan. It seemed like this divorce was happening no matter what, and I just needed to get used to it.

34

Camille

I had never felt like such an outsider. But with the way I'd been acting lately, I guess you could say I *was* an outsider. After Alexis went back home with her parents, we pretty much went our separate ways. First, though, I asked Jasmine, Angel and even Tyeesha to forgive me. While Tyeesha and Angel didn't hesitate, Jasmine had this look like too much damage had been done.

"Camille, I'm just really through with you," she said. Then she recited some crazy saying her grandma used to have about "Fool me once, shame on you. Fool me twice, shame on me." I asked my mom what it meant, and she said it basically meant that if you give a person a chance to do you wrong after they've already done it once, it's your fault.

That hurt my heart. I think I really messed up this time. But Tyeesha didn't think so.

"What you guys have is special. Don't give up without a fight," she told me when she called to invite me to Angelica's second birthday party.

I didn't want to go and get my feelings hurt, but Angel told Miss Rachel it was okay for me to come. She had taken it upon herself to invite me when Angel told her she wanted me there but couldn't bring herself to call me.

So here I was, clutching a pink gift bag closer as I debated my next move.

"Hi, Camille," Miss Rachel said as she came up behind me.

"Hi."

"Why are you waiting out here?" she asked. I was standing on the porch of Angel's house, debating whether I should go in.

I shrugged as I stared at the front door. "They don't want me here, I know it."

"Did they actually say those words?"

"Not exactly, but I know."

She gave me a sympathetic look. "I think your guilt may be playing a role in that. As I seem to recall, Angel said you could come if you want."

"Well, regardless, I don't want to get all embarrassed. I've had enough of that to last a lifetime."

Before I knew it, tears were trickling down my cheeks. I dabbed at my eyes, trying to get myself together.

"Camille, nobody is perfect. Everyone makes mistakes. The key is to learn from those mistakes." Miss Rachel's voice was soft and gentle, but it still didn't ease the pain I was feeling.

"Why would they even want to be my friends anymore?" I asked. That's what I'd been wrestling with all night. "I said some horrible things."

"Because they love you," she replied. "And love means sometimes forgiving."

"Even if they forgave you once before?" I said, thinking about all the drama that had gone down with the teen talk show. I'd been a jerk then, but I had been an even bigger jerk now.

"Yes. Sometimes even again."

"So, do you think they'll forgive me?"

"I think they've already forgiven you."

"Even Jasmine?"

Miss Rachel laughed. "Jasmine might take a little work. But, Camille, you can't keep doing your friends wrong and expect them to always be there when you're ready to make it right. Growing up means *learning* from our mistakes, not repeating them."

I sniffed. "I know. I just got caught up. But I realized, all the fame in the world doesn't mean anything if you don't have people who really love you and care about you there to share it with you."

"I couldn't have said it better myself." She took my hand. "Come on. Let's go see the birthday girl. And your friends."

Miss Rachel knocked on Angel's front door. I wanted to turn and run, but I knew I couldn't let my pride get the best of me.

"Knock, knock," Miss Rachel said, easing the front door open when no one answered.

The laughter that filled the room faded when I walked in. Actually, only Alexis, Angel, Tyeesha and Jasmine stopped laughing, but it felt like the whole room got quiet. In all, about twenty people had been invited, including some people I assumed were Angel's relatives. Angelica was sitting at the head of a small table. She was dressed in the prettiest pink party dress and was surrounded by eight other little kids.

"Aunt-ie 'Mille!" Angelica yelled. She jumped down from the table and came racing over toward me.

I picked her up and kissed her forehead. "I two," she said, holding up two fingers.

"I know, pumpkin. Happy birthday."

"Mine?" she asked, pointing to the bag hanging on my arm.

"No, this is *my* Dora the Explorer bag."

She giggled as she squirmed trying to get down. "Mine! Dora!"

I gave her the bag, and she immediately tore into it, pulling out the Dora doll. I noticed Angel glancing sideways at Jasmine, like she was hoping Jasmine didn't ruin her daughter's birthday.

Angelica didn't notice as she raced off to show her friends the doll. I spoke to Angel's mom and a few other people before walking over to Alexis, Angel, Jasmine and Tyeesha.

"Hi, you guys," I said shyly.

Tyeesha was the only one to respond. But I was determined. "Alexis, how are your parents?" I asked.

"Getting a divorce," she said coldly. I could hear the pain in her voice. She was about to go through an awful time, and I wanted more than anything to be there to help her.

We stood in awkward silence before I finally said to Angel, "I didn't know if Angelica had that doll or not."

"Umph," was all Jasmine said.

"Thanks," Angel replied. "She didn't."

"You know, girls, I think it would be a good idea if you all went outside and talked," Miss Rachel said, easing over to us.

"I'm sure Camille just came to drop off her gift," Jasmine said. "She has to get back to her real friends."

It dawned on me then that they only knew what they'd read in the tabloid. They didn't know the real story behind my getting fired, or the fact that I didn't have anything to do with Sisco and his crew anymore.

Angel finally spoke up. "You guys, let's go outside and talk, because I'm really tired of this. It takes too much energy for us to stay mad at each other. And I don't want all of this negativity up at my baby's birthday party."

The forcefulness in her voice made us all do double-takes. Tyeesha seconded her. "I'm with you, Angel. Let's just go outside with Camille. End this and move on. I finally found some decent friends, and I can't take all of this bickering. Come on, Camille."

I didn't protest as she took my hand. She reached for Jasmine's hand, but Jasmine popped a cupcake in her mouth and didn't move.

Tyeesha rolled her eyes and shook her head. "We're going outside whether you like it or not. So stop being stubborn." She all but pulled both of us toward the door.

We soon gathered at the back of Angel's porch, no one saying a word. "Well?" Tyeesha said after no one started the conversation.

"Well what?" Jasmine asked.

I decided to finally speak up. They didn't have to ever forgive me, but I needed to have my say.

"I'm sorry. I'm so, so sorry," I began. "I'm sorry I wasn't there for you, Alexis. I'm sorry I acted like a complete jerk, and I'm sorry I got caught up. I let all of this stuff go to my head."

"You ain't never lied," Jasmine tsked.

"Would you let me finish? Please?" I said. This was hard enough without all her comments.

Jasmine smirked but didn't say anything else.

"When you guys tried to bring me back to reality, I felt like you were trying to steal my joy. But what I know now is that you all were trying to keep me grounded. I got caught up in the drama. I lost Xavier because of it. But that's okay—boys come and go. But friends like you guys last a lifetime. And I want to do whatever it takes to get that back." I felt the tears coming, and this time I didn't try to stop them from falling.

Angel looked at me, her expression soft. "Camille, we have been through so much. You know we're your friends. But you hurt us with your ways."

"I know. And if you never forgive me, just know that I'm sorry." I sniffed.

She sighed heavily. "We forgive you. Don't we, Alexis?"

Alexis was watching me with tears in her eyes as well. I wanted to jump for joy when she nodded.

"Jasmine?" Angel said, turning to her. "We forgive her, right?"

Jasmine didn't respond.

"Come on, Jas. Don't be like that," Angel said.

"So we forgive her this time, then what? The next time something else comes up, she'll kick us to the curb again."

"No, I won't. I promise."

"Come on, Jasmine. When your brother died, Camille was there for you from the very beginning. And Alexis, Camille has always had your back." Angel tilted her head toward the house. "Miss Rachel is always talking about forgiveness. It's time we started listening."

I guess the compassionate tone in Angel's voice touched all of us.

"Jasmine?" Angel asked again.

"Okay, fine, whatever," she said, throwing up her hands.

It was a start. Jasmine was the toughest of the bunch. I'd have to try a little harder to make things right with her, but I was willing to do whatever it took.

I was about to say something when Marcus, Angelica's father, stuck his head out the back door. A tall, handsome, brown-skinned boy stood next to him.

"Hey, I'm about to go," Marcus said. "My friend Juan is here to pick me up," he said, pointing at the boy next to him.

"Hey, Juan," Angel said.

"What's up, girl?"

"Are you sure you're okay with me bailing?" Marcus asked Angel.

"Naw, you're good. You've been here all day and you did pay for the party." I know Angel was happy about that. Up until a few months ago, she couldn't even get Marcus to acknowledge that Angelica was his.

"Cool, we have tickets to the VIP section of Jay-Z's party, and you know everybody's going to be there," Marcus said.

"Hey," Juan said, cocking his head and looking at me. "Aren't you Camille Simone? That singer from Sisco's video?"

Even though I didn't say anything, Marcus nodded. "Yeah, that's her."

Juan smiled widely. "Dang, girl, you're tight. You oughta roll with us. I got an extra ticket." He started bouncing on his toes. "Beyoncé might be there, and my brother works on her security team. I can get you back to meet her. You never know. She might be able to help you with your singing career."

Meeting Beyoncé! Oh, that would be so off the chain. The thought was enticing, but I glanced over at my friends, who were all looking like they were waiting to see what I would do.

"You got four extra tickets?" I finally asked. "I mean, five," I said, noticing Tyeesha. She smiled.

"Five?" Juan said, drawing back. "These tickets are one hundred and fifty dollars a pop."

"Then I think I'm going to pass."

"What?" he said, looking at Marcus. "Did you hear me say Beyoncé might be there? And even if she isn't, you can meet some pretty important people to help with your singing career."

"Naw, not really feeling the singing thing."

"There's bank to be made," he said, shaking his head like I was the craziest person he'd ever met.

I glanced around at my girls again. The expressions on all of their faces told me they were proud of me. But even more so, I was proud of myself.

"Maybe so," I told him. "But what I have here, that's priceless."

"Awwww," Angel said, coming over to hug me. My other friends joined her as I heard Juan mumble something about me being "crazy for throwing away a singing career over some broads."

I didn't care what he was talking about. As I stood there in a big group hug, I knew friendship was more important than fame. I'd learned that the hard way. And now that I'd been given a second chance, no way was I going to mess it up.

Reader's Group Guide

Caught Up in the Drama

ReShonda Tate Billingsley

Description

Camille enters a talent show to showcase her amazing voice at the urging of her boyfriend, Xavier, which surprises her three best friends. She blows the crowd away, and then gets a surprise herself: not only does she win the contest (and the prize money), but she also snags the lead role in superstar Sisco's new music video. Fame hits Camille like a tidal wave, and soon she is swept up in the chaos and drama that comes with being a celebrity, drifting further and further from her friends and her boyfriend. One friend in particular, Alexis, really needs her help: her parents' fighting has escalated and they're heading toward divorce, but Camille is too caught up with her new friends and extracurriculars to pay attention. At her wit's end and trying to save her parents' marriage, Alexis comes up with a plan to unite her parents in a family "tragedy" by running away. When her friends come together again to bring Alexis home, they finally confront Camille about her betrayal of both the group and herself.

Questions for Discussion

1. Camille's newfound fame goes straight to her head, and fast. Why do you think this is? How can Camille be so quick to accept this new lifestyle and leave her friends behind? How do you think you would act if you were in her shoes?

2. Alexis's parents are fighting more and more, and things at home are becoming very stressful. How does Alexis cope? Have you or your friends had to deal with a divorce? How did you handle it, or help your friends do so?

3. How do the girls respond to Camille's new attitude, and how does Camille react to the girls? How do you think that reflects each girl's personality and her individual friendship with Camille?

4. Camille's boyfriend, Xavier, breaks up with Camille after seeing her kiss Sisco while taping the video. Do you think he was justified in doing so? How did Camille and Xavier each mishandle their argument? Discuss how communicating and being more honest with each other might have affected their relationship.

5. Camille knowingly gets into trouble with her mother because of the outfits the producer makes her wear, and especially because of Sisco's aggressive sexual behavior. How could Camille have been more assertive in protecting herself? Could she have done so without jeopardizing her role in the video? What choice would you have made in Camille's place?

6. A new girl, Tyeesha, becomes part of the Good Girlz when Camille is absent. How do the other girls immediately judge her, and why? How does she prove herself in their eyes? Have you ever judged someone based on appearance, only to discover that they are different than you expected? Explain.

7. Alexis thinks that her parents' divorce is her fault, and that she can fix it. Do you think that her solution to the problem made sense? Do you think she would have made such a rash decision if Camille had answered her phone call? When Alexis runs away, we see her interact with her old friends for the first time in this book. How is their friendship dramatically different than the one she has with the Good Girlz?

8. Camille lies to the Good Girlz when she falls in with a new group of friends, even when Alexis is in obvious need of her shoulder to cry on and her best friend to talk to. Why do you think Camille is influenced by these new girls, even though they use her? Why does she trust them more than the Good Girlz?

9. What causes Camille to finally realize that she has abandoned her friends? Why do you think it takes her so long to change her ways? Do you think she has really learned her lesson this time? How does she prove that to her friends?

10. Alexis, Angel, and Jasmine have a difficult time accepting Camille's apology. Have you ever found it hard to forgive a friend? How can they move past what has happened among the four of them?

11. The girls have known each other for a very long time, and yet Camille's fame still threatens their friendship. At the end of the book, how has each character matured, and do you believe their friendship has become stronger?

Activities to Enhance Your Book Club

1. Many women featured in music videos today are ignored or disrespected. How do you think these videos influence the perception of women? Discuss with your group what you can do to empower yourself as girls and women. Discuss your favorite videos, songs, and singers that recognize women as strong and intelligent.

2. The book kicks off with a talent show in which Camille shocks her friends with her talent—they knew she could dance, but they had no idea she could sing! Arrange a talent show with your friends and show off your secret talents.

3. *Caught Up in the Drama* is the sixth book in the Good Girlz series. If you haven't already, read several of the others and discuss the series and the characters as a whole. How does each girl develop and grow? How does reading more of the books help you to understand the characters and their actions more thoroughly?

Don't miss the next Good Girlz adventure

Drama Queens

Coming Fall 2010

Turn the page for a sneak preview of
Drama Queens . . .

Angel

College life was off the chain! At least that's the way it seemed as I looked out across the courtyard of Prairie View A&M University. There were people everywhere, laughing, talking and just hanging out. Most of the people were watching the Kappa Alpha Psi fraternity do an impromptu step show.

Our recruiting guide said it was called "Hump Day on the Hill," a time when all the students come together, dance, listen to music and just socialize. They even had a deejay showcasing his newest music.

"It's Wednesday and we like to celebrate to help get through the week," our guide, a petite, pretty brown-skinned girl named Lauren said. She was leading us and about twenty other students. "We do it every week, except finals and dead week." The girl turned to smile at Miss Rachel, the sponsor of the Good Girlz, our community service organization. Miss Rachel had arranged this campus tour after me and the other four Good Girlz, Camille, Alexis, Jasmine and Tyeesha, expressed interest in visiting again. We'd come about two months ago and I think all of us were sold on coming to this college after we graduated in a few months. "And don't worry, it's not all fun and games," Lauren said. "We wrap up Hump Day on the Hill with a prayer or a spiritual song."

Miss Rachel nodded her approval. Personally, the prayer was all-good, but right about now, just seeing the groups of people mingling was enough to make me know I'd made the right decision—Prairie View was where I wanted to be. We had all applied after our first visit, when we'd come to the campus for a Girls, Inc. conference. So far, none of us had received acceptance letters, but I knew after today we all wanted to go here now more than ever.

"Girls, you all enjoy the show, I'm going to run inside to the restroom," Miss Rachel told us.

We waved as she walked off, before turning our attention to a fraternity called the Que Dogs, who were stepping in gold boots and had dog collars around their necks. It was all pretty entertaining, then, out of nowhere, we heard, "So, you ladies enjoying the tour?"

I looked up to see the cutest guy I'd ever seen in my life. He was about six feet tall, sandpaper-brown with deep dimples and a head full of curly hair.

"We are," Camille said, immediately moving over to shake his hand. Camille Harris was the boy-crazy one of the group. She batted her eyelashes at him and my heart sank. That meant she was about to get her flirt on so he'd be off limits to me. Not that he'd even want me anyway. I was the shy one out of the five of us. I'd been told I was cute—this one guy even said I looked like a younger version of the singer Shakira—but the fact remained, I had a two-year-old daughter. These college boys probably wouldn't want anyone with kids.

"That's nice," the guy said to Camille. "I'm Rico. My friends call me R-Train." He adjusted his backpack on his shoulder. His smile made my stomach flutter. He had on a PV T-shirt and some tan cargo shorts.

"And I'm Camille." She pointed at us. "These are my friends, Jasmine, Alexis, Tyeesha and Angel."

We all waved, except for Jasmine. She was being her usual grouchy self. She'd just gotten through complaining about how hot it was, even though I could tell she was enjoying the campus tour.

Rico reached out as if he was trying to take Camille's hand. She smiled coyly as she stepped forward.

"It's a pleasure to meet you . . ." Rico stepped around Camille and took my hand. ". . . Angel. Is that what she said it was?"

My eyes widened in shock. Jasmine and Tyesha busted out laughing. Embarrassment covered Camille's face but Rico didn't seem to notice or care.

"So where are you ladies from?" he asked, still holding my hand.

"Umm, we're from, ah, we're from Madison Hi—"

Alexis immediately cut me off. "We're from Houston. Just checking out the school." She shot me the evil eye. I'd forgotten our pact that we weren't going to let people know we were still in high school during our tour. Although I didn't see what the big deal was, everyone on the tour was from a high school.

"Houston?" He nodded. "So, you're right down the road?"

I couldn't do anything but nod back.

"So that means if I wanted to see you again, I would only have a forty-five minute drive." He looked at me like we were the only two people standing in the courtyard.

"Yeah, um . . . w-we . . . " I couldn't believe I was acting like I was a blubbering fool. He was going to think I was so lame.

Jasmine, who, thankfully, knew me very well, stepped to my aid.

"What makes you think she wants to see you again?" Jasmine said, removing his hand from mine. I was glad she was smiling so at least she wouldn't scare him off. At six feet tall, with an athletic build, it wasn't anything for Jasmine to scare someone off.

"I don't know if she does want to see me. But I'd really like to see her again," he said, still staring at me.

I was completely speechless. And for once, so was Jasmine. I think she was waiting on him to run some type of game, but when he didn't—he just stood there looking at me with those piercing gray eyes—she didn't know what to say.

"Seriously, I think you're beautiful," he told me. "And no, I don't know anything about you. You might be a serial killer." He broke out in a big smile. "But I sure would like to get to know you."

"So you know that you'd like to know her even though

you don't even know her?" Alexis asked, her hands planted firmly on her hips.

We all turned to stare at her. For all of her money (Alexis came from a filthy rich family) Alexis couldn't buy a decent line. My girl was corny as all get out.

"Actually, I do," Rico said, not looking the least bit confused.

"Well, handle your business then," Tyeesha said, stepping up and playfully pushing his shoulder. She was the newest one to the Good Girlz and had fit right in. Her joking kind of broke the mood and we all laughed.

"Why don't you let me give you a private tour?" Rico said, gently reaching out, taking my hand again and pulling me toward him.

Jasmine snatched me back. "I don't think so, Brother Man. *You* could be the serial killer."

He laughed. "You're right. I wasn't thinking." He dug in his backpack and pulled out a piece of paper. "Let me give you my cell phone number. I live here on campus, but it's nothing for me to swoop down to Houston and pick you up. So give me a call. Maybe we can get to know each other over the phone—first. Then you can let me give you that private tour."

"Unh-unh," Jasmine said, wagging her finger. "Ain't gon' be no private tours. We don't know you like that."

"That's why I'm giving her the number." He scribbled his number on a piece of paper then handed it to me. "So she can get to know me *like that*." He winked. "Angel, I await your call." He blew me a kiss before walking off.

I tried to keep it together so I didn't appear to be a total geek, but I wanted to jump up and down and do a happy dance.

"Girl, you better call him," Camille said, genuinely excited for me. I had thought she was going to be bothered since he'd dissed her.

"You don't want him?" I asked. Yes, he was cute, but that was one thing the Good Girlz didn't do was talk to someone else's man. Camille, Jasmine, Alexis and I had been tight since joining the Good Girlz two years ago. Tyeesha joined a few months ago, but she had worked her way into our circle like she'd been there all along.

Camille waved me off. "Please, you know how I do. I was just flirting. Besides," she playfully wiggled her neck, "even if I did want him, he obviously only has eyes for you."

"Who was that?" We all looked up to see Miss Rachel peering off in the direction where Rico had walked off.

"That's about to be Angel's new man," Alexis sang. "They call him R-Train."

"Like the subway?" Miss Rachel asked, shaking her head. She didn't wait for anyone to answer as she wagged her finger our way. "What have I told you girls? You don't need to be worried about any boys, men or anything else."

"Oh, Miss Rachel, it's natural, human nature," Camille joked.

"I got your human nature," she replied. "I told you where having boys on the brain will land you." Miss Rachel readily admitted that, like Camille, she used to be boy crazy as a teen and she'd had more than her share of trouble behind it. She'd started the Good Girlz after marrying a preacher and deciding she wanted to keep young teenage girls from making the same mistakes that she made.

"Yeah, yeah, yeah," Camille said, albeit respectfully. We'd all heard this speech before. And although she didn't act like it, Camille had come a long way. She'd actually come to the Good Girlz behind a boy named Keith. He'd broken out of jail and Camille was hiding him in her grandmother's house. She didn't know he'd broken out of jail, but when the police rolled up on them playing house, Keith bolted and left Camille to take the rap for "harboring a fugitive." The judge let her come to the Good Girlz instead of keeping her in juvenile detention.

Truthfully, we'd all had our share of boy drama, including me. I got pregnant at fifteen. And don't get me wrong, I'm not promiscuous. In fact, that was my only time. And as much as I love my daughter, Angelica, I definitely could've waited to have her because being a teenage mom was no joke.

Thankfully, Angelica's father, Marcus, had come around. It took him two years, but he was now a part of Angelica's life. He and I were cordial, but that's about as far as it went. We'll never get back together. I think part of him still resents me for having a baby, like I did it all by myself.

"Angel got his number and everything," Tyesha said, snapping me out of my thoughts.

"How old is that boy?" Rachel said, frowning.

We all shrugged.

"I don't know," I finally said. "It's not like we got into a whole bunch of details."

"Well, he looks old to me," Miss Rachel said.

"I'm not even thinking about him," I said. I just wanted to get the spotlight off of me. I had every intention of calling Rico. I just didn't want Miss Rachel all up in my business. It wasn't every day that someone as cute as Rico showed an interest in me. And I was at the point in my life when I was ready to show him some interest right back. Shoot, I was graduating in two months and I didn't even have anyone I could take to the prom.

"Good," Miss Rachel said. "I didn't bring you all up here to this school to pick up guys." She looked over at Lauren, who appeared to be saying good-bye to everyone. "Well, girls, the tour has wrapped up. Dr. Breyer would like to meet with you ladies in her office."

We made our way back across the campus to the vice president's office. I wondered why we were going to see her, but Miss Rachel was moving so fast I couldn't really ask any questions.

"She doesn't really have anything to do with enrollment," Miss Rachel began, "but her husband and my husband play golf together. So she wanted to meet you personally."

We made our way across campus and into a nicely decorated office. A large photo of a panther hung on the wall and there were photos of happy-looking college kids everywhere. The furniture looked worn but the whole office seemed like it was student-friendly.

The secretary ushered us back and we all took a seat around Dr. Breyer's large oak desk. She greeted us with an enthusiastic smile. A tall, pretty woman with a warm and friendly face, she reminded me more of a grandmother than a vice president of a college.

After some brief introductions, she said, "Well, girls, I don't have much time because I have to get to a meeting, but I am so proud of what Rachel has done with the program and I wanted to personally give you these."

We all looked confused for a moment as she handed each of us an envelope. We turned them over, still looking confused. Miss Rachel stood in the background, grinning like she was crazy.

I was the first one who tore into mine and all I saw was congratulations. "Oh, wow," I said. Camille, Jasmine, Alexis and Tyeesha all ripped theirs open at the same time and they, too, squealed in delight.

"Yes, congratulations are in honor," Dr. Breyer said. "Prairie View A&M University would be very honored if you all would attend."

"We've been accepted?" Tyeesha asked.

"Like there was ever any doubt," Alexis sang.

"Maybe not for you," Jasmine replied. Alexis was a brainiac, but the rest of us struggled from time to time.

"Of course, this is contingent upon all of you actually graduating," Dr. Breyer said. "Judging from your records that should be no problem."

Jasmine looked like she wanted to say something but decided against it.

"Thank you," we all said together.

"No, thank you, ladies. And I look forward to a personal relationship with each one of you," Dr. Breyer said.

"Lorraine, thank you so much," Miss Rachel said. "You just don't know how much this means to me and the girls."

"Yes, it means a lot," I said. I couldn't actually believe I was going to college. My mom had already said she would keep Angelica because she wanted me to further my education. But the reality that I might really get to go didn't set in until just now.

"Well, we need to get back down the road." Miss Rachel stood up. "I wanted to get the girls home before it got too dark."

We all stood and shook Dr. Breyer's hand and we practically floated out of the room. I couldn't wait to get home and tell my mom. I would be the first person in my family to go to college so I was definitely excited. Then add to the fact that I had met a cute college boy, well, things couldn't get any better than that.

Want more teen fiction fun?
Check out these titles: